A Young Boy's Scary Stories

Scary Adventure Stories For Boys

By Donald Kirk

1964

SWEETWATER STAGELINES™
SAN ANTONIO, TEXAS

Scary Adventure Stories For Boys
By Donald Kirk

Transcribed from six books written
by Donald Kirk in 1964

STORY SUMMARY:
A series of science-fantasy tales of gruesome deeds.

Published by
SWEETWATER STAGELINES™
An imprint of
THE OLD WEST COMPANY™
5118 Village Trail Drive
San Antonio, Texas 78218

Tradepaper (ISBN13): 978-0-9898004-8-8
Printed and bound in the United States of America
R5

Scary Adventure Stories For Boys

By Donald Kirk

In this book you'll find A six-volume set of stories for young readers written by a sixteen-year-old for his two younger brothers. They were transcribed exactly as written in 1964 with few modifications for this special edition. The stories were also changed from Present Tense to Past Tense. The original books were illustrated with simple pencil illustrations by the young author, and the text was typed on an Underwood typewriter—he had just learned how to type in high school. His books were seven inches wide by three inches high with a staple binding and each book had about fifty pages. All of his "Books" are now presented in this one delicious volume.

The publishers hope you enjoy these fantastic, thrilling, and scary stories. And as you read these stories, draw your own pictures of the monsters.

CONTENTS

RATE THESE 13 STORIES
As You Read Each One
1-THE WORST (Circle In Pencil Only) THE BEST-10

The No Longer Top Secret Story

1 2 3 4 5 6 7 8 9 10

The Man That Never Lived

1 2 3 4 5 6 7 8 9 10

The Protozoan Invasion

1 2 3 4 5 6 7 8 9 10

Who Has The Corpse?

1 2 3 4 5 6 7 8 9 10

The Transit Eye

1 2 3 4 5 6 7 8 9 10

Dissolving Goo

1 2 3 4 5 6 7 8 9 10

The Pecan Pickers

1 2 3 4 5 6 7 8 9 10

Inky Business

1 2 3 4 5 6 7 8 9 10

Mr. Graves and the Suitcase Murders

1 2 3 4 5 6 7 8 9 10

The Myocardiograph

1 2 3 4 5 6 7 8 9 10

Mucous Membrane and the Medium

1 2 3 4 5 6 7 8 9 10

Milkweeds and Mustard Gas

1 2 3 4 5 6 7 8 9 10

Monster Mushrooms and More

1 2 3 4 5 6 7 8 9 10

The No Longer Top Secret Story Of The Invisible Man

By Donald Kirk

CONTENTS

The incredible story of the Invisible Man began in the summer of 1960 in New York City when a quiet man, fascinated with science, accidentally discovered a frightening fact: a mixture of his special alloy MX3109 with $C_{12}H_{22}O_{11}$ (plain sugar), and a small amount of hydrogen monoxide, will, when added to the Thyroid gland of an animal, cause the animal to become invisible. Yes, invisible! So with that in mind, read on about the man who would soon become invisible.

THE NO LONGER
TOP SECRET STORY
OF THE INVISIBLE MAN

CHAPTER ONE

This would-be scientist, Jack Carter, did not know if this mixture would produce a harmful or unanticipated effect to an animal, so, for six months, he kept his discovery a secret while experimenting with this mixture he called KRIKNOD. He gave small amounts of KRIKNOD to laboratory rats, to birds, and to small monkeys, taking note of their responses. Some of the animals became invisible while others did not. He put red tags around the necks of his invisible lab animals so he could see where they were in their cages.

Finally, on November 13, 1960, Jack Carter—thinking he knew as much as he needed to know about the KRIKNOD drug—drank an ounce of the bubbling purple-colored liquid himself.

But what Jack Carter didn't know—and would never know—was that this would be the first step toward terrifying the entire world. So, stay tuned for Chapter Two and see what happens.

Now for Chapter Two. . .

CHAPTER TWO

Jack Carter became invisible as expected, but he did not know what to do. He ran from his laboratory and started up the stairs to his bedroom, but as he reached the thirteenth step, he tripped and fell because he was unable to see his feet.

"I can't see my feet!" he yelled. "How am I going to climb the stairs?" It was apparently hard for him to climb stairs.

Jack Carter eventually made it up the stairs and rushed into his bedroom. He looked into the vanity mirror and saw nothing. No image at all! He was definitely invisible. He had to tell someone about his discovery. But how? They wouldn't be able to see him!

"Oh, I've got it."

Jack Carter took a roll of white bandaging tape and wrapped it around his head but left holes in front of his eyes so he could see. He left small holes in front of his nose so he could breath and left an opening for his mouth so he could speak...and eat. Wrapping up his head, it was now possible for him to be seen. He got dressed and put on his shoes—he could now see his feet—and wore gloves to hide his invisible hands. And finally, he put on a hat to hide his invisible noggin.

Jack Carter prepared to drive into the mountains to tell a scientist about his awesome discovery. He walked carefully back down the stairs, got a sample of his KRIKNOD, locked up the house, and climbed into his car. He then sped off as if he was in a hurry. He was excited, to be sure, about his new discovery.

Ready for Chapter Three? . . .

CHAPTER THREE

Three hours later Dr. Carter arrived at the mountain cabin of his scientist friend.

"What? Who are you?" asked the scientist as he opened the door. "Were you in some kind of accident?"

(You might be interested in knowing that the scientist's name was Dr. Kilmore.)

"No, I'm fine, It's me Jack Carter, you know me, a long-term friend."

"Well, it does sound like you, but what is

this all about?"

"I've made a great discovery! I'm invisible! Look into my eyes. You see, there's nothing there, no eyeballs, no brain matter visible! You can see the bandages on the back of my head, can't you?"

"Yes, very, very strange."

"Here, let me take off my gloves," said Jack Carter as he removed his gloves.

Dr. Kilmore's eyes widened; he was totally dumbfounded. "How…how is this possible?"

"Here, I'll show you. In this bottle is KRIKNOD."

"KRIKNOD?"

"Yes, a special formula that will make any mammal invisible when it is digested."

Dr. Kilmore's eyes glared at Carter. "Give me that," he said as he grabbed the bottle from the doctor. "Where is the formula for this?"

"I have it hidden where no one can find it, no one, not even you!" cried out Carter.

"We could do a lot with this discovery," insisted Kilmore. "We could do fantastic things. Ha, we could get rich, very rich. Bank robberies would be a cinch."

"No, no," screamed Carter, "I will not use my discovery for criminal activity!"

"Yes you will, or else," said Dr. Kilmore as he pulled a gun from his desk drawer. "Where is the formula? Tell me now!"

"I won't tell..."

BANG! BANG!

Dr. Carter's bandaged body fell limp to the floor. He was apparently dead.

What now? Find out in Chapter Four...

CHAPTER FOUR

Several hours later, Dr. Kilmore—after burying Jack Carter in his back yard—drank the bottle of KRIKNOD. He then left his cabin headed for Carter's home. The car looked as if it was rolling down the highway without a driver because Dr. Kilmore wasn't wearing bandages. He was invisible! When the car without a visible driver reached Carter's house, it came to a stop, the door opened, and then it closed. If anyone had seen that, they would have thought they were mentally off their bean.

Anyway, the glass in the back door of the house suddenly shattered, the latch came undone, and the doorknob turned. The door opened, and then closed. Dr. Kilmore was now in the house, still invisible.

He searched the house, opened drawers, pulled pictures off the wall, and overturned just about everything. But he was unable to find the formula. So, frustrated and upset, he left Carter's house, concerned and angered.

What do you think is going to happen next? Do you know? We don't know because there was no record of it, BUT we do know what happened a week later, on the 19th of November:

There was a big bank robbery and guess who did the robbing...yes, that's right...it was Dr. Kilmore! He stole two-hundred-fifty-thousand-dollars and no one saw him do it! It was "easy as pie" to rob the bank: the vault door was already open!

Then, every week on a Friday, there was another robbery. And after two months, Kilmore's robbery record was five banks and three department stores. The whole world was beginning to hear about the never-seen thief. The police tried to keep watch on everything that could possibly be stolen.

Now move your eyeballs to chapter FIVE...

CHAPTER FIVE

Now we go to Police Headquarters in New York City:

"Chief, what are we going to do? This robber, who we've never seen, walks right past our guards."

"Yes, it doesn't do us any good to watch over anything. What, or who, is completely invisible. He doesn't wear clothes and there are no footprints. That's what the witnesses tell us."

But then one cold wintry day: *Crunch-crunch-crunch.* Someone reported hearing a crunching sound and saw footsteps appear in the freshly fallen snow, one right after the other.

"It must be an invisible MAN because the feet are quite large," said the Captain.

"Hey," said one of the bank owners, "we can put a trip wire around the snow banks. When the Invisible Man touches the wire, an alarm will go off."

"But he could see it?"

"Not if the wire were placed just below the surface of the snow so he wouldn't know it was there."

"Good idea, we'll do it," replied the Captain.

Meanwhile, way down in Texas, another scientist, a Mr. Sam Bottoms, was working on a formula for making a skin cream that would also make a man invisible. "I've got it!"

He's got what? Find out by reading Chapter Six…

CHAPTER SIX

He's got a formula, that's what: $x3+9L=74-y5$. Sam Bottoms mixed up a large quantity of this skin cream, put it in bottles, and then took a train to New York City. He went immediately to police headquarters.

"I want to show you something, Chief," said Bottoms, excitedly. When I put this cream on my skin, the epidermis seems to disappear. When I cover my whole body with it—which I can wash off at any time—I become invisible to the naked eye. Several of your policemen could make themselves disappear, and then follow the Invisible Man's footsteps without being seen.

"By George, another good idea. We might now be able to find his hideout!"

"Oh, and Chief, have your men shave their heads and use the cream on their noggins. We wouldn't want floating hair to give them away."

"Good idea."

Stay tuned for Chapter Seven…

CHAPTER SEVEN

Two nights later, one of the trip wires sent out an alarm. Two of the invisible cops—with their bald heads—rushed to the bank where the alarm had come from.

Two pairs of eyeballs appeared at the Second National Bank, no visible body, just eyeballs floating through the air! A strange sight indeed.

"Hopefully Joe, he's still inside the bank."

"You go around to the back door and I'll watch the front," said Officer Pete.

"Got it."

"Oh, and Joe, close your eyelids if he looks in your direction. Then he won't see your eyeballs."

"Got it."

A few minutes later, the Invisible Man came out the back door leaving tracks in the snow. Joe followed him, his eyeballs moving eerily through the air. He followed the Invisible Man's footprints up a hill.

Suddenly, as Joe neared the top of the hill, he fell into snow that covered a deep hole.

The bank president came running out of the bank, "We've been robbed!"

"Its okay, we got a man following him," whispered Officer Pete.

But a long time passed, and Joe didn't return.

"Get a search party looking for Joe," commanded the Chief of Police.

"He's got to be up on the hill."

"But he's going to be hard to find."

"What? Why?"

"All you're going to see in the snow is two marbles!"

"Oh."

Sadly, two hours later, they found Joe frozen to death.

CHAPTER EIGHT

On March 7, 1961, another mysterious robbery took place, but this time it was in London, England! Five people were injured, and a half-million dollars stolen! People were becoming very frightened by this invisible man. Wouldn't you be scared of something you couldn't see… and might hurt you? I would. People all over town decided to stay in their homes and keep their doors and windows locked.

Scotland Yard was doing its best to find this

invisible robber. At the police station, this conversation was going on:

"Let's see, gentlemen, what do we know about this Invisible Man?"

"He usually robs on Friday nights and has no problem hurting people."

"Oh, and he's only going after the big money now, no penny-anti stakes for him."

"That means we won't have to watch the small businesses."

"Hey, I've got it, a way to catch him—a way to SEE that crook!"

"How?" asked the chief as he sat up in his chair, very interested.

"We can put a bottle of liquid aluminum with reflective dust above the doors of the bigger banks. When the Invisible Man enters a bank, the door will knock the reflective material on him."

"But what good does that do us?" asked the chief.

"When the liquid aluminum dries on him it'll be possible for us to see him when we shine a flashlight on him!"

"It's worth a try," said the chief.

Guess what? Chapter Nine is on the next page. So, go to page 13, quick!

CHAPTER NINE

Meanwhile, back in New York City, a police-man was searching through Dr. Kilmore's lab at his mountain cabin. Do you know why? It was because the car he used at one of his rob-beries was found at the cabin and the police figured it was the Invisible Man's home...so they began searching it.

Outside of the cabin, another policeman called out, "Come here Lieutenant Perkins, freshly turned-over soil! Something's been buried here recently."

"I'll get us some shovels."

When Perkins returned, the two policemen started digging.

"*Clang*," they hit something.

"Look, a dead man with no arms!"

"My word!"

Two hours later after the armless man had been taken to the morgue, Lt. Perkins noticed he was now missing just one arm!"

"Get the Captain down here right quick!"

Captain Morgan hurried to the morgue.

"Look Captain, this dead man had NO arms when we found him, but now he's missing only one arm."

"I think this was another invisible man, but

now he's beginning to reappear."

"Yes, look, you're right, the remaining arm is starting to show itself."

"Captain…Captain," yelled a policeman running into the morgue. "The dead man's name is Jack Carter and he lives, or did live, at 413 West Milam."

"Let's go see what we can find at his house."

STOP! Stop reading now and go take a break. Go get a cold drink of water or a glass of milk; there's a lot more exciting story to go!

CHAPTER TEN

Captain Morgan, Lt. Perkins, and another policeman went to Carter's home. They forced the lock and opened the door.

"Look, a science laboratory! A very big, scary-looking, chemistry set: test tubes, Bunsen burners, flasks, all that kind of stuff."

"I bet this Carter fellow discovered how to make himself invisible, but then the now Invisible Man stole the formula for it."

"And killed Jack Carter."

"We've got to search every inch of this lab. There's bound to be something here that will help us track this killer."

Back in London it was now a cold, dreary night, but unfortunately, there was no snow on the ground that could leave footprints.

And then, all of a sudden, there was a shuffling sound and people started yelling. Several policemen began to shine their flashlights around the area.

They saw a big, silver-colored man run down the street.

"That's him, the Invisible Man! Get him!"

The strange-looking silver creature ran into a dark alley, but two policemen were staying close behind.

"Stop or be shot!" yelled one of them. The cop fired his gun and the Invisible Man grabbed his leg. He was hit! It slowed him down considerable.

The cops caught up, cuffed him, and hauled him off to the hoosegow.

Was this the end for the Invisible Man? Is this the end of our story? Keep reading and you'll find out…

CHAPTER ELEVEN

The no-longer Invisible Man was put in a jail cell with bright lights, and two guards with flashlights sat outside the cell. The Invisible

Man could be seen because of the reflective aluminum still stuck to his body.

"Hey cops, can I get a glass of water? I'm awfully thirty."

"I guess it would be all right."

Late that night, when the two policemen were falling asleep on the job, the Invisible Man secretly washed off the aluminum using the water he got from the guard.

In the morning, a policeman tried to bring the Invisible Man his breakfast.

"He's...he's not here, he's gone!"

"He has to be in there!"

"We don't see him," screamed the terrified guards as they shone their flashlights into the jail cell.

"Give me the keys, I'm going in."

One of the guards walked into the cell and felt around for the prisoner moving carefully from one corner to the next.

"He's not here! Go tell the Captain!"

"Do I have to?"

"Yes, now get going!"

How did the Invisible Man escape?

That's right, you guessed it: he moved around as the guard searched for him and easily slipped out the cell door.

The sneaky Invisible Man walked out of Scotland Yard headed for the nearest airport. He, of course, didn't need a ticket for a flight to the United States; he just walked calmly onto the plane because no one could see him.

Several hours later, when the plane was over the Atlantic Ocean, Dr. Kilmore—the Invisible Man—walked to the cockpit and knocked out the co-pilot. He told the pilot HE was the Invisible Man and returned to the back of the plane. The pilot saw the door open and close, and figured he was gone, so he quietly radioed the New York airport that the Invisible Man was on board, and they should be ready to take him into custody when they landed.

An hour later, Dr. Kilmore returned to the cockpit and sat down in the co-pilots seat. When the plane approached the shores of the United States, Kilmore took the controls and put the plane in a dive. The pilot pulled on the stick, but something was holding it down. He didn't know it was the Invisible Man!

The plane spun out of control and crashed into the cold Atlantic sea!

What now? Is the Invisible man finally dead? Go on to Chapter Twelve to find out.

CHAPTER TWELVE

No, he wasn't dead. Dr. Kilmore climbed out of the sinking plane and swam to shore. The rest of the people in the plane drowned.

The next day, the newspaper reported the plane crash and said there were no survivors. They reported that the Invisible Man was on board and that he too probably died. They said this because, as you know, the pilot had called the tower and said he was on board.

Two weeks later, on a Friday, after the country thought there would be no more robberies or killings by the Invisible Man, five railroad men died. This is how it happened: a freight train was traveling at sixty-miles-per-hour when the caboose came uncoupled. It soon rolled to a stop, and then began to roll backward down a steep grade. But it went off the track, tumbled down a cliff, and crashed into a river!

But do you know who uncoupled that caboose? Yep, it was the Invisible Man! No one knew the accident had been caused by YOU KNOW WHO! So, on the next Friday, a thirteen-car passenger train tumbled into a raging river when the bridge they were crossing collapsed!

Now, move your eyeballs to the next chapter if your eyelids haven't covered them over yet.

CHAPTER THIRTEEN

Dr. Kilmore made some adjustments on a special pair of glasses.

"I think it's time I start making a lot more money," said Kilmore as he headed for the Third National Bank of New York.

"If any of those invisible cops come around me again while I'm at work, I'll be able to see them with my infra-red glasses."

Dr. Kilmore walked into the National Bank, walked behind the teller's cages and walked into the big money vault. He put the loot into a cloth bag from behind the counter and walked out the front door.

Then, suddenly, he tripped and fell to the ground. A loud alarm went off and search lights shone down on him. With his infrared glasses, the Invisible Man saw the invisible guards coming after him, but he calmly and quietly got up and climbed into his car and sped away.

Two cop cars chased after him. The three cars raced for miles up a mountain road. Just as they reached the top of the mountain, the brakes in Kilmore's car quit working and his car started going faster and faster and faster down the hill. The brakes wouldn't slow the car down!

Kilmore then noticed that the invisible skin cream was wearing off. He could see his hands and his face in the rearview mirror. The car was going much faster now and the road was next to a steep cliff. And it was a long drop.

"This is the end for me," said Dr. Kilmore as he turned the steering wheel wildly.

The police were still trailing several miles behind, obviously unable to go as fast as Dr. Kilmore. The doctor screamed as the car broke through a guardrail and fell off the cliff! There was a long silence, then crunching metal, and then a big explosion. Dr. Kilmore was dead.

Several hours later, at the bottom of the cliff, the police—and everyone in the vicinity—were standing around looking at the famous Invisible Man who was no longer invisible. Dr. Kilmore had hurt many people and stole millions of dollars. And on Friday, May 13, 1961, the badly burned body of the Invisible Man was lowered into a grave and dirt thrown on his coffin.

THE END

By the way, you might be interested to know the money stolen by the Invisible Man was never found, so it just might be buried in your backyard right now! Oh, and the next time you rub a lotion on your skin, make sure it's not that Invisible skin cream!

—This story was written by Donald Kirk in November of 1963 when he was 15 years old.

SCARY ADVENTURE STORIES FOR BOYS

The Man That Never Lived (His Name Was ZORBA)

By Donald Kirk

CONTENTS
The Man That Never Lived

This story could not have happened without a Fourth Dimension. And I cannot prove it ever happened, because only a few people knew of this scary science experiment that I'm going to tell you about.

In 1948, there lived—and still lives today—a small, short and stubby man that went by the name "Albert Proton." No one knew of the research laboratory he had hidden in his dark basement. But now you can know of it if you turn the page and read on…

THE MAN THAT NEVER LIVED

CHAPTER ONE

On one dark, dreary night Albert Proton finished making a small red pill. But it wasn't an ordinary pill as you will soon find out. Proton knew of a woman that was about to have a baby—and without her knowing—he had her swallow this very special red pill.

When she had her baby, she never saw it. Why? Because, the baby disappeared into nothingness immediately after it was born! That's right, disappeared as soon as it was born. The doctors could not figure out where the baby had gone.

Nine years later, in 1957, Albert Proton, an amateur wanna-be scientist, walked down the stairs to his basement laboratory. He walked to a large closet, opened the heavy door, and rolled out a machine that looked like a complicated pile of wheels, pulleys, belts, and gears. He pulled a chair up to the contraption, sat down, and began to push buttons, turn knobs, and flip switches. Lights flashed on the machine. It rattled crazily and made a strange humming sound.

"Ah," said Proton, "it's time for me to communicate with ZORBA in the Fourth Dimension. Come in ZORBA. Come in please."

An image came up on a big screen over the computer.

"Are you ZORBA?" asked Proton. "You do not know me. I am Proton."

The computer whirred and a blue light flashed.

A deep haunting, electronic-like voice came over the loud speaker in a very slow tone, "You-have-a-lot-of-ex-plaining-to-do-Albert-Pro-ton."

"Yes, I'm going to explain it all to you now."

"Ex-plain."

"You were born nine years ago here on planet Earth…"

"But, I-am-old-er-than-that!"

"Yes, I know. You're twenty-seven years old now. You age three times as fast as we Earth people."

The red and yellow lights on the computer flashed as Proton explained the whole story to ZORBA: "An Earth woman was your mother, but immediately after you were born, you vanished from Earth and went into the Fourth Dimension."

"But-why?   Why-was-I-not-born-like-a-normal-Earth-creature?" asked ZORBA with an unpleasant, agitated voice.

"I gave your mother a very special red pill that I made. A pill that would, by changing your molecular makeup, send you immediately into another world; not the three-dimensional world we humans on Earth live in. Now listen carefully."

A green light flashed.

"I also put into that special pill some of the knowledge you now have. I did this, ZORBA, because you would not encounter the Earth language anywhere in the Fourth Dimension and thus, would not be able to talk to me now."

All the lights flashed.

"Have I told you everything you want to know?"

"Yes, except-for-one-thing."

"What's that ZORBA?"

"Why?"

Chapter two is continued below.

CHAPTER TWO

"Why?"

"Yes, why?" The red and yellow lights flashed wildly.

"Well, because I have plans for you…"

The Man That Never Lived

Bleak-bleak-whirr-swirrrrr—The screen image went haywire with zigzag lines, and then it went out of focus and the scary creation stopped shaking. All the lights went out.

Proton stood up, pushing his chair back, "It must have blown a fuse."

The next day, Albert Proton decided to tell his cousin, Leonard Neutron, about the Fourth Dimension, and about his new creation: ZORBA.

"You've got to help me with this project. It will be a great addition to our scientific knowledge."

"I'm not so sure, but I will help you."

Late that night, Proton put new fuses in his strange machine and contacted ZORBA. Proton explained the project to him. ZORBA understood and agreed to the undertaking.

It was now TWO MINUTES before MIDNIGHT, three day later. Proton and his cousin Neutron were in the basement laboratory. ZORBA, with bushy white hair and very large round eyes, was in focus on the big screen.

"Everything is ready here. Are you ready there, ZORBA?"

"I-am-read-y."

Proton flipped several switches on his contraption and set several dials. One dial was set to the words PUMPVILLE NEVADA.

"It's midnight!" called out Neutron.

Proton pushed a green button.

At that moment in Nevada a whole deserted town was blown up—blown to smithereens! All the dilapidated houses were turned to kindling.

The next day, the front page of the newspaper told of a deserted town in Nevada that was suddenly blown to bits without cause. There had been no one living there and there was no electricity and no natural gas that could have caused the explosion.

"It worked!" cried Proton with a wide grin. "It worked just as planned."

Albert Proton immediately called some of the well-known scientists in the country. He told them that a fourth dimension did indeed exist, and HE could contact it.

"I can prove it," he said. "That deserted town, Pumpville—the town that blew up the other day—well, it was no accident! And tomorrow, another town will blow up. If you men are in the hills outside Tanktown, Nevada tomorrow at midnight, you'll see the explosion."

"Okay, we'll be there."

"Good."

It was now MIDNIGHT the next evening. Proton set the machine location dial to read TANKTOWN. He pushed the green button.

But something happened, I mean didn't happen. The town didn't blow up! Nothing occurred! I wonder why? Continue to Chapter Three to find out.

CHAPTER THREE

The scientists came to Proton's laboratory.

"So you're one of those eggheads who thinks he can do anything, even blow up a town when you're thousands of miles away. That's nuts!"

"I have done it! I have contacted the Fourth Dimension. I have worked on this all my life. I've finally done it."

"You're off your rocker, Proton!" blurted out one scientist. They climbed the stairs out of the basement and left Proton to his insanity. They left thinking this Albert Proton may have gone completely insane. But they weren't sure. The explosion of Pumpville may have been just a coincidence. Who knew?

After the scientists left, Proton rolled his machine out of the closet. He sat down at the console and got in contact with ZORBA.

"ZORBA, frequency 67256 Delta, come in."

ZORBA came into view on the big screen in front of Proton.

"I'm-here-Al-bert-Pro-ton. You-called-me?"

"Why did you NOT blow up Tanktown in Nevada?"

Lights flashed on the machine. "I-do-not-want-to-use-my-powers. I do not want-the-scientists-to-find-out-about-the-fourth-dimension."

"Why not?" asked Proton.

"Then-the-whole-world-would-know."

"But we made a deal. You agreed to help further my scientific research!" blasted the little man.

"Yes, but-I-have-changed-my-mind."

"But…"

"If-you-tell-any-one, any-one-at-all, about-the-Fourth Di-men-sion, you-will-be-de-stroyed-like-that-Ne-vada-town!"

"But, but, I don't under…"

"Ha, ha, you'll-never-find-the-Fourth-Di-men-sion. I-just-may-be-be-side-you-right-now …and-you-can't-see-me. Ha, ha!"

Bleak, bleak, blip, swirrrr—

The machine became quiet.

"Just my luck to pick a stubborn baby for my experiment. ZORBA is stubborn and determined to have his way, no matter what. That could be dangerous."

Guess what, Chapter Four follows below, so keep on reading right fast...

CHAPTER FOUR

Proton didn't take ZORBA'S warning seriously, so left his basement laboratory for the home of an old friend who was also a scientist. Proton believed he could convince his friend Dr. Dabble that there really was a Fourth Dimension he could contact because the Doctor worked with him on a past Fourth-Dimension research project...although that project ended in failure.

Proton reached the home of the fellow scientist, and after a long discussion, his friend agreed to come to Proton's lab.

The two men got to Proton's house and started down the basement stairs. But, without warning, Proton felt a shock in his legs and he lost his balance...and fell down the stairs.

But he wasn't injured too badly. He appeared to be okay.

"What happened?" asked Dr. Dabble.

"I don't know, I suddenly felt a tingling shock and lost control of both my legs! But I'll be all right. Here, I must show you this machine."

Proton went over to the closet containing his invention. He touched the door handle. "*Ahhh-*

hhh, it shocked me! The handle shocked me!"

"I'll open it," said Albert's friend.

"No don't, it'll shock you."

But Dr. Dabble went to the door anyway, and as he started to touch the handle, it came loose and fell to the floor!

The scientist friend tried to open the door without the handle, but he couldn't; he couldn't open it!

(The two men didn't know it, but the past few incidents had been what you might call Fourth Dimension Voodooism. ZORBA was causing the incidents because he didn't want Proton's friend to find out about the very special contact machine in the closet.)

"I'll go get something to pry the door open, you stay here," insisted Proton as he climbed up the basement stairs.

A few long minutes passed.

A few more minutes expired.

And many more minutes flew by.

What could have gone wrong? Move your eyeballs to the next chapter to find out.

CHAPTER FIVE

Dr. Dabble got restless and hurried upstairs. He walked into the living room but saw that no one was there. He looked in the bedroom, no one there. He walked into the kitchen, and there, he saw something on the floor: it was Albert Proton lying on the floor in a puddle of water. Also in the water was a frayed electric wire from a toaster. He had been electrocuted, shocked to ever-lovin' death! Proton was toast...burnt toast!

Several week later, after the funeral, Leonard Neutron, decided to use cousin Proton's machine to contact ZORBA.

He rolled out the diabolical machine and flipped on the necessary switches and adjusted the dials.

"ZORBA of frequency 67256 Delta. Do you read me? Come in please."

"This-is-ZORBA. Why-do-you-contact-me?"

Leonard Neutron replied, "I have reason to believe that you have other abilities besides blowing up deserted towns."

"Yes...I-do."

"In some of my cousin's scientific notes, it said that you might have the power to stop time here on Earth."

Yes-that's-right. I do have that power. Right now, I can make everything on your Earth stop completely…and no one would know it was happening."

"Could it be possible," asked Neutron, "to have everything stop EXCEPT one person?"

"I believe so, with the proper equipment."

After about an hour of discussion with the strange big-eyed entity on the large screen, Neutron made a deal with it. ZORBA promised not to change his mind if Neutron did something for him.

So, for the next few weeks, Neutron worked on a small pocket-sized gadget. ZORBA told him, step by step, how to put it together. Finally, Leonard Neutron finished building the strange little gadget.

The next evening, Neutron went to the house of the scientist that had helped his cousin work on the previous Fourth Dimension project, but, before he walked onto the porch, he pushed a red button on his pocket gadget. EVERYTHING AROUND HIM CAME TO A SUDDEN FRIGHTENING STOP! The birds stopped chirping, the leaves on the trees stopped fluttering, the cars on the streets all came to a stop, and people walking along the sidewalks stopped in their tracks, frozen in place. Everything stopped. The light breeze stopped blowing. The whole world came to a halt!

Neutron opened the front door and entered the house. There, in the living room, was Dr. Dabble sitting in his chair looking at his newspaper, BUT his head was stone still. Everything happened as you would normally see it, except for one thing: the scene was like a photograph, but a three-dimensional one. NOTHING WAS MOVING! The clock on the wall had stopped at the exact moment Neutron had pushed the red button. Neutron looked out the window. There was a bird that had stopped flapping its wings in mid-flight, just hanging there frozen in mid air, a very strange sight. Even the clouds in the sky had stopped moving!

After Leonard Neutron got over the shock of this new world—completely silent and unmoving—he began to search through the files of Dr. Dabble. He was looking for all the information he could find on the Fourth Dimension. After searching through many files and pulling out anything he could find on the Fourth Dimension, Neutron looked through the rest of the house.

Several hours passed and Neutron had gathered all the information he could find. As he left the house, he saw the bird still suspended in the air. A strange sight indeed!

Neutron returned home and threw all the information about the Fourth Dimension in his fireplace. He lit it—it quickly burned to ashes.

Leonard Neutron then returned to the basement and contacted ZORBA.

"Yes, Neutron, now that you've done what I've asked of you, you can do as you wish with the pocket gadget that stops time."

The machine *bleaked, blipped, spat, swirrrrrred*, and then turned itself off.

Leonard Neutron headed for the First National Bank, taking the pocket gadget with him.

What on Earth was he going to do? Stay tuned for the next exciting chapter.

CHAPTER SIX

Neutron arrived at the bank and walked in. He then pushed the red button on his pocket gadget.

EVERYTHING STOPPED. The clock stopped. The customers stopped. The tellers stopped.

Neutron moved over to the open vault and grabbed several bags of dough, lettuce, cabbage, ice, mullah, and even some money! He casually walked out of the bank and returned home where he put the bank's money in a secret cavity in a wall of his house.

Neutron then again pushed the red button, and that started the world moving again.

Every day for the next few weeks, Neutron robbed a different bank, but he only took some of the money in each financial institution hoping they wouldn't miss it right away. On Friday, after putting his latest stolen loot in the wall of his house, he went to a tavern. He sat down at a table and ordered a root beer, but then he had what he thought was a better idea.

"I've an idea," announced Neutron, excitedly. "I'll have me several drinks...on the house! Ha hah." He took out the pocket gadget.

But just then, a drunk walked by and grabbed the gadget from him. "Hey, what ya got here, Sonny?' asked the drunk.

"Hey, give that back to me. Don't push that..."

But the drunk pushed the red button.

EVERYTHING CAME TO A STOP...EXCEPT THE DRUNK!

"Hey man, what's going on, speak to me," said the drunk to Neutron as he grabbed him. "What Mister? You don't like my company?"

Neutron, of course, isn't able to answer. His

face was stone stiff, eyes fixed on the drunk.

The drunk dropped the gadget in his coat pocket. "I…I must have had too much to drink, uh, no one is moving."

The drunk wobbled off and out the front door.

What will happen to Neutron now? He was up a big creek without a paddle, without his gadget! Stay tuned for chapter seven.

CHAPTER SEVEN

The drunken man wondered into an alley and fell to the ground next to a bunch of trash cans. He fell fast asleep.

The next day, on a Saturday, he awakened to find himself in an alley. Nothing new for him, but he also found something strange in his coat pocket.

"Hey, what's this?" he said to himself.

He looked it over, flipped it upside down, and saw the red button…BUT WOULD HE PUSH IT?

The only way you can find the answer to that question is continue to the next page and read chapter eight.

CHAPTER EIGHT

Yes, he did push the red button! But then he threw the gadget into a garbage can.

"Some drunk musta put it dare in my pocket," said the man as he walked off, still wobbling like a sailor on a ship in the high seas.

Back in the tavern, Neutron began to move again, "Give it here, you drunk! What? Where, where have you gone? He has the pocket gadget. I've got to find him!"

Neutron hurried out of the tavern and looked all over town for the drunk. He went to all the saloons. He checked all the street gutters. He looked in Dumpsters. There was neither hide nor hair of him. Finally, Neutron went to the police station and told an officer that a drunken man had stolen from him a black box of valuable electronic equipment. He described the man's appearance as best he could. The police on the street, and those in patrol cars, kept an eye open for the drunk during the rest of Friday, but they never could find him. Who knows where he wandered off to?

Finally, several days later, the police found a man that fit the description.

"Yeah, but I didn't steal it, no sir. I found it in

my coat pocket."

"Sure you did," said the policeman.

"I did, I swear it!"

"Then, what did you do with it?" shouted the cop. "Think man, clear those cobwebs out of your pickled head."

"I...I, oh, now I remember, I threw it in a garbage can...I think!"

"You think? Where? What garbage can?"

"In an alley."

"In what alley?"

"Next to a tavern."

"You've got to be kidding! There are hundreds of saloons in this town. Take us to the one YOU THINK you were in Friday night...or Saturday morning."

They all took off trying to find the right tavern. When the drunk was sure he was at the right place, they looked in the trash cans, but...

"Oh no, the garbage men have already been here!" blasted Neutron.

The policeman tried to calm him down, "You'll never see that black box again Mister; the city dump is big, very big, quite big. Sorry we couldn't help you."

The next day Neutron—still mad about loosing the pocket gadget—decided to contact ZORBA.

STOP! HALT! STOP! Stop here…

Now that you've stopped, you can go on to the next chapter…

CHAPTER NINE

Neutron pushed buttons, turned knobs, and flipped switches.

"ZORBA in the Fourth Dimension. Come in ZORBA. Frequency 67256 Delta, come in."

ZORBA came onto the big screen.

"I guess you know, ZORBA, that I lost the pocket gadget.

"Yes, I-know, but-I-cannot-tell-you-what… *Bleak, sput, swirrrrr—clang.*"

The machine began to rattle very badly and as it shook, parts fell off. Then, all of a sudden, the machine exploded, parts flying everywhere. Leonard Neutron was thrown to the floor. The house caught on fire. And it burned, and burned, and burned, until there was nothing left but a bare slab of concrete.

THE END

At the beginning of our story, I said Albert Proton was still living today. Well, he is! After he was apparently shocked to death in his kitchen, he was transported to the Fourth Dimension to haunt someone he knew!

By the way, you might also be interested to know that a pocket gadget that can stop time in its tracks may still be somewhere in your city garbage dump! But I don't recommend trying to find it in that stinky mess...but maybe, by chance, it'll turn up. Some dog might find it, but I hope he doesn't bite down on the red button! He he.

Stay tuned for the next exciting book: Book Three: The Protozoan Invasion & Who Has the Corpse? Two great stories in one book.

—Donald wrote this story from Jan 17th
through Jan 20th 1964
when he was 16.

The Protozoan Invasion
&
Who Has The Corpse?

TWO SCARY STORIES IN ONE BOOK!

By Donald Kirk

CONTENTS

The following two short stories are weird, strange, gruesome, and maybe a little bit funny. Can you handle them? If you can, I dare you to read on.

Now turn the page…

1. THE PROTOZOAN INVASION

CHAPTER ONE

One night, at about two-o'clock in the morning, a woman woke up because she heard something strange outside. She sat up in her bed to look out the window, screamed in terror, jumped out of bed, and rushed from the bedroom still yelling. Her face looked as white as a newly-washed bed sheet. She ran down the hall, out the front door, and hurried down the street in her nightgown...still screaming her lungs out!

Meanwhile something was crashing through the bedroom window...

WHO IS IT? OR WHAT IS IT?
Continue reading to find out . . .

In another home, in the same neighborhood, a man who went by the name of Mopbucket, was running to get his shotgun. He must have seen something too, BUT WHAT?

Mopbucket rushed down the basement

stairs with his shotgun. BANG! BANG! He shot at a huge worm-like creature moving across the floor. The creature crawled onto the basement furnace and wrapped around it. Mopbucket stood there watching the slimy animal as it started to steam and sizzle. It then slowly dropped to the floor and flattened out like a pancake. IT HAD APPARENTLY DIED!

But what was this monstrous worm?

The frightened man examined the green snake-like creature that was at least ten feet long! Holy moly! But now, it was just a long pancake.

The next day, Mopbucket took the city bus to a research laboratory. It turns out he was the janitor of the building. He asked one of the scientists working there to come to his house and look at the strange creature he found in his basement.

And so, that afternoon, at Mopbucket's home, the scientist said, "I've never seen anything like it in my life! Well, actually it looks a lot like a protozoan."

"But a protozoan is invisible to the naked eye," said Mopbucket.

"That's right, you'd need a microscope to see one."

"But, oh man, I can SEE this one, and I'm NOT looking through a microscope!"

"I know. Scary isn't it?"

The big microscopic creature was hauled to the laboratory for examination. Dr. Microbot, a microbiologist, did some research on the giant creature. He soon came to the conclusion that it was, indeed, a protozoan. But a very big one! He also found out that this particular protozoan is a EUGLENA DESES, a species that lives in mud. Oh, yuck!

Hey, don't stop reading. The story isn't over yet. It has just begun. Keep reading. Don't you want to find out what happens next? To find out you'll have to go to the next chapter...

CHAPTER TWO

The telephone in the science lab rang. A lab assistant answered it. After a few minutes listening, the assistant hung up and went to Dr. Microbot's office.

"Doctor, the police chief just called. He said a frightened man who lives in Mud Creek (a nearby town) called him and said they were being invaded by giant worms that were crushing people."

Dr. Microbot asked, "Isn't Mudcreek near the delta of a river?"

"Yeah?"

"A muddy delta?"

"Yeah, very muddy."

"Oh no," said the microbiologist, "I'm afraid those giant worms are Euglena Protozoa that have come out of the mud and have grown to enormous size."

"That's obvious, but HOW did they get so big?" asked the assistant.

"Who knows, maybe some chemical change in their bodies, or maybe in their environment."

"The only thing we can do now is get help from the military," declared Dr. Microbot.

Mr. Mopbucket, who had been mopping the floor, spoke up: "The army, the navy, the air force, they won't do any good, sir. Bullets will go right through a protozoan and not harm it because they're one-celled creatures. I ought to know, the other night when I shot the protozoan in my basement, it wasn't harmed at all."

"Then how did you kill it?" asked the doctor.

"I didn't. The thing crawled onto my basement furnace and there it died, flattened out like a pancake!"

"It makes sense, a protozoan can't live if there is no moisture present. When the protozoan in your basement touched that hot furnace, the moisture was sucked from its body."

"So, doctor, to get rid of these creatures all we have to do is dry them up."

"It would seem so."

CHAPTER THREE

It was raining cats and dogs outside (and other creatures), and the slimy protozoan continued to invade Muddy Creek and other towns along the river. But soon, over radio and television, there came a special news bulletin: *Everyone must evacuate the city. Take only the absolute necessities with you. Leave the rest behind. Everyone must leave Muddy Creek immediately!*

It wasn't long before the streets were jammed with cars, and people, and cats & dogs (it was still raining) and the giant protozoan slithered through town; their worm-like bodies expanding and contracting like an accordion in order to move. Some of these creatures climbed up on buildings and shimmied up telephone poles where they sometimes dropped on top of cars, smashing them to smithereens.

"With this rain, the protozoan will really be increasing in number," declared Dr. Microbot as he opened his desk drawer and took out a chart with illustrations on it. "This chart shows the steps in the process of an Euglena Protozoa as it divides into two protozoan, each becoming another animal. The first picture shows a single Euglena before it has divided. In the second picture, the gullet is dividing and the creature has almost been duplicated. In the third picture, it has nearly finished dividing. After it has broken into two protozoan, each of those will divide into two more, and those four into eight more, and sixteen more, and so on. That is why we must stop them NOW!"

"As I said before, we'll have to figure out a way to take away their moisture," said Mr. Mopbucket.

"But we can't with all this rain," declared Microbot's assistant scientist.

"Look, the window!"

They all look over in the direction of the window and what do you think they see?

YOU'RE RIGHT! They see a giant slimy-green protozoan crashing through the glass.

"Let's get out of here!"

"Follow me," yelled Dr. Microbot, "into this empty room."

The three men ran into the room and the protozoan followed them there!

Uh oh, it looked like the three men would be crushed to death by the slimy creature. Find out what happens in the next chapter.

CHAPTER FOUR

The three men ran through the room and out a back door. They locked the door behind them. Mr. Mopbucket ran around to the front and locked the other door to the empty room.

THE PROTOZOAN WAS TRAPPED!

All of a sudden, several big lights went on in the room. And after a few minutes the protozoan flattened out on the floor…like a pancake.

"You did it Doc, you did it, he's dead! The heat lamps have dried him out!"

"If we could only do that on a large scale," wondered Mr. Mopbucket.

"That's it! On a large scale, sure, I've got it!" cried the doctor. "We'll do this…" The doctor told them his plan.

"It'll work," said Mopbucket, "Its got to work!"

"I'll hunt down all the searchlights I can," said the assistant.

"And I'll get the gasoline and the matches," added Mr. Mopbucket.

"We'll meet you on the north side of town at the grass field…in two hours," said Dr. Microbot.

"Hey look! It looks like our luck is changing; the rain has stopped! Maybe our luck has finally had an upturn."

The two hours quickly passed. On the south, west, and east sides of Muddy Creek, bright searchlights were turned on. Each of the protozoan tried to get as far away as they could from the hot carbon-arc lights. The only direction the giant protozoan could move was to the north of town. And so that's the way they went. The sun was also now shining brightly. The protozoan crawled into the vast grass field just north of town.

All of a sudden, the grass burst into flames and burned real fast.

An hour passed and all there was left to see, as far as one could see, were piles of dead, dried-up Euglena Protozoa. But this didn't solve the town's problem. They still had to stop more protozoan from growing into giant rippling creatures. BUT HOW COULD THIS BE DONE? They didn't even know what was causing them to grow so very big.

Find out how by continuing to read this story. In case you don't know, Chapter Five is on the next page.

CHAPTER FIVE

Dr. Microbot went down to the river's delta to get a specimen of the gooey mud and bring it back to the lab to examine it. After several hours of study, he found that something had been added to the mud…and it looked like it might have been a man-made chemical. After separating the chemical from the mud, he determined that it contained a waste product from a paper mill.

The doctor quickly made a trip to a paper mill on the shore of the muddy delta. He found out they were putting a chemical into the paper to make it harder to tear and harder to dissolve in water. He asked the foreman, "Where do you dump your chemical wastes?"

"There in that muddy river flat," he answered.

"Then you must stop production immediately! If you don't, we'll have protozoan slithering over this whole county!"

The foreman shut down the mill and Dr. Microbot analyzed the chemical. He ran an experiment with some microscopic protozoan in a culture dish (a flat, glass dish for growing bacteria). The doctor discovered that when the chemical comes in direct contact with the Euglena Protozoa, it causes them to grow, and grow, and grow! He also found out that diluting the chemical with large amounts of water would make it completely harmless.

The next day the dry riverbed was flooded with water diverted from another river. And during the next few days, all the protozoan growing in the mud flats were killed off and the place looked like a big pile of pancakes on a huge griddle. The citizens of Muddy Creek could finally come back to their homes.

"Well," said Mr. Mopbucket, "case closed!"

THE END

2. WHO HAS THE CORPSE?

CHAPTER ONE

Rap-rap-cling-cling-chink.
"Now Jake, push!"
A large stone with the name "LORD JACOB III" chiseled on it fell to the ground.
"Look Sam, we've done it!"
"Yeah, Jake, bring the wagon up."

Jake and Sam stood in a dark, scary graveyard on a foggy, dreary night. And all the shadows seemed to be moving, ready to grab you. The moon was full, and two men had just opened a stone casket. They lifted out the body of a decomposed man: an ugly smelly corpse! They then threw the corpse onto a buckboard pulled by two horses.

Then, out of the blue, the two men heard a noise in the bushes and…

"Get your hands up, you thievin' grave robbers! Turn around and walk over to that there stone coffin."

They did, smartly.

"Now get in, the both of you, get into the tomb," demanded a tall well-dressed man with black top hat as he pointed a flintlock pistol at the two men. Now turn around."

When they did, the tall man hit the two grave robbers over the head with his pistol. They fell limp into the stone coffin. The stranger hopped up on the wagon and, "giddy-up," he rode out of the cemetery.

The stranger drove the wagon down a dusty dirt road that ran across a desolate, mesquite-covered desert. It was not long before he arrived in a small western town. He pulled up in front of a tiny, one-room shack with a sign that read: DOC BONES—BULLETS REMOVED FOR A SMALL FEE.

The stranger got out of the wagon and unlocked the front door. He then hauled the corpse into the little building and dragged it into a back room. The stranger—who must have been Doc Bones—took off his long, white coat, rolled up his shirtsleeves, and opened the glass door of an instrument cabinet. He took out a long knife and large forceps, and carried them over to the corpse.

WHAT IS HE GOING TO DO NOW?
Keep reading to find out.

CHAPTER TWO

Straight off, Doc Bones suddenly fell to the floor, unconscious. There were two men standing above the doctor: Jake the Vulture and Cemetery Sam, the two grave robbers Doc left behind at the cemetery. They picked up the corpse and carried it out to the buckboard, but when they climbed up on the wagon, the two wheels on the right side fell off and the wagon tilted on its side. The corpse rolled quietly onto the ground and the grave robbers ran after the two wagon wheels rolling down the street.

Seeing this, a little, four-foot-tall man snuck up to the buckboard and dragged the corpse into a nearby alley. He then put the smelly body on a donkey and lead the donkey away.

"Are you ready, Cemetery Sam, 'cause here

he comes…NOW!"

Jake and Sam pulled on a rope that tripped the donkey AND the little man. The little man fell and hit his little head on a little rock that knocked him a little bit bonkers. He shook his head trying to knock his brain back in place. The corpse was thrown off the donkey. Jake and Cemetery Sam dragged the corpse back to the wagon, replaced the wheels, and drove off.

By now, you are probably wondering why everyone wanted that smelly corpse. Well, you'll have to keep on wondering, because the only way you can find out is to go to Chapter Three.

CHAPTER THREE

Jake and Sam drove the wagon up to an old wooden shack in the hills and carried the corpse into the shack. And out from behind the door came Doc Bones!

"Drop that, ooh, that stinking body, and put your hands up, now!"

The two grave robbers dropped the body, but as they did so, they knocked Doc's old pistol out of his hand. This started a fight as everyone went for his gun. The table and chairs were broken into pieces of kindling, and the corpse was kicked around and stepped on more than a couple of times.

About this time, the county sheriff walked in on the brawl...and he had a gun in his hand.

"Stop this ruckus, or I'll shoot," he called out firmly.

They all stopped and raised their hands high in the air.

"Ooh, what's that smell? Hey, what's this body on the floor?"

"Well, Sheriff, we were just having a little argument, and he got hit over the head with a chair," declared Jake the Vulture.

"The sheriff put his gun away and bent over to look at the body on the floor. Sam wasted no time grabbing a chair and hitting the Sheriff over the head with it. He dropped to the floor out cold. Doc Bones raced out the front door and jumped on his horse, but Jake and Sam ran after him and pulled him off the horse. They took him back into the shack.

"Look, Jake, look! The body is gone!"

"Someone has taken it! It ain't here no more."

"Well, we still got the Sheriff."

"And we got ol' Doc here."

"Tie Doc up," ordered Jake. "When the Sheriff comes too, he'll take Doc to jail. So let's go find the thief who took our corpse."

CHAPTER FOUR

Meanwhile, a man was dragging the corpse through the bushes behind the shack. And it wasn't the little man, but another, much bigger man. The man's name: Turkey Creek Johnson. He put the corpse on his horse and tied a bandanna over his own mouth and nose. I guess the smell was getting to him too. He galloped off down the hill and into the valley and found a nice shady spot under a mesquite tree where he took the corpse off his horse. Turkey Creek Johnson pulled out a large knife from a holster strapped to his leg and made a long, deep cut into the dead body's belly. Turkey Creek then reached into the stomach of the corpse and pulled out something: a pearl necklace! He reached in again and came up with a large diamond ring! Yes, really!

"Wow, I've hit a gold mine!" said Turkey Creek as he reached into the gooey guts of the ghastly corpse one more time and came up with a diamond-studded horse collar! Yeah, a very BIG horse collar! How Lord Jacob the Third could have swallowed that was a real mystery! Just imagine him trying to swallow it.

When Turkey Creek was satisfied that there was no more jewelry in the stomach, he took his needle & thread—the one he used to sew buttons on his shirt...and stitched back together the hole in the corpse's stomach. Turkey Creek Johnson slung the body back on his horse and rode off, stirring up a nice trail of dust. He rode back to the shack in the hills.

At the shack, Turkey Creek took the corpse inside and found the sheriff still unconscious and Doc Bones still tied up. Turkey Creek left the corpse in the shack and rode off.

About an hour later, the Sheriff awakened and saw the corpse on the floor and Doc Bones tied up. He untied the doctor and then surprised him by snapping handcuffs on him!

"You're going to the jailhouse, Doc...for killing this man on the floor."

"Me! I didn't kill any..."

"Quiet! Get on my horse."

The two men rode back to town.

And then, Jake the Vulture and Sam Cemetery returned to the mining shack, went in, and were surprised to find:

"Hey, the Sheriff and the Doc are gone!"

"And the corpse has returned!"

"Something strange is going on around here," said Cemetery Sam.

"I don't care. Give me your knife."

Jake cut open the corpse and reached into

its stomach. He pulled out a heavy piece of paper and unfolded it. On the paper was written: HA HA! YOU'RE TOO LATE. I'VE BEATEN YOU TO THE JEWELS! HA HA!

"We've been outsmarted again!" declared Jake.

"I don't believe this! Who got our jewels?"

"Maybe Doc knows something," replied Cemetery Sam. I'll go talk to him while you take this corpse back to the graveyard. He's really stinking up the countryside. Besides, he deserves a good-night's rest after what he's been through."

Jack soon arrived at the cemetery with the smelly corpse and placed it back in the stone coffin. But he was unable to replace the heavy stone lid. He climbed back on his wagon seat, but just then...

Five men jumped out of the bushes, all with guns pointed at Jake."

"Well, well, so this is our grave robber!"

Jake was bold, jumped behind the stone coffin, and pulled his pistol. The five men jumped for cover and gunfire popped in every direction. *Bang-bang. Bang-bang.*

CHAPTER FIVE

While all this shooting was going on, Cemetery Sam was sneaking up behind the jailhouse. He peeked into the small barred window.

"Doc, you in there?"

"I'm here. Is that you Cemetery Sam, the grave digger?"

"It's me."

"I'm gonna tan your hide!"

"Doc, hold on! Do you know what happened to the corpse?"

"What do you mean?"

"How'd he get back in the shack?"

"I just might know."

"Then, do you know who took it?"

"I might...but you'll have to get me out of this dirty jail cell before I tell you. It's full of nasty vermin."

Cemetery Sam thought for a moment and then said, "Okay, I'll get you out."

Sam went to the front of the Sheriff's office, went in, and said to the deputy sitting at the desk, "Deputy, I need to see Doc, I think I've broken my arm!"

"He's indisposed."

"I'm hurtin' somthin' fierce, Deputy!"

"Okay, okay, come with me." The deputy got up and turned toward the jail door. Sam quickly pulled his pistol, hit the deputy over the head, got the jail key, unlocked the cell door, and let the doctor out.

"Okay, tell me Doc, who took the corpse!"

"It was Turkey Creek Johnson, the farmer."

As the two men left the Sheriff's office, the Sheriff showed up, "Stop you two!"

Doc tried to run.

The Sheriff shot Doc in the leg, but Sam got away by ducking into an alley.

What's going to happen now...if anything? Continue reading to find out.

CHAPTER SIX

The posse's jail wagon was coming down the street with a wounded man locked behind its bars. Why, it was Jake the Vulture! His head was all wrapped up in white bandages. You see, a heavy stone coffin lid had fallen on him!

Cemetery Sam was now headed for Turkey Creek's farm. When he arrived at the farm-house he went inside and shot Turkey Creek squarely in the foot! Turkey cried out in pain and limped out the door. Sam took the pearl necklace, diamond ring, and diamond-studded horse collar. He then went to a jewelry shop in another town and tried to trade the jewelry for cash money.

"Here, how much will you give me for this pearl necklace, diamond ring, and diamond-studded horse collar? They look great don't you think? A matched set!"

"Hum, they look good alright, but I reckon they're only worth about two dollars."

"TWO DOLLARS!" screamed Sam.

"Yes, that's all."

"But why? They're pearls and diamonds!"

"I'm sorry, they're not real."

"Not real?"

"Well, don't you know, this is just cheap costume jewelry, it's just glass!"

THE END

Below is a list of the men that were injured because greedy men will do anything for a little money:

* There was the little man that hit his head on a rock.

* There was old Doc Bones who was shot in the leg so he couldn't run.

* There was Jake the Vulture who had a stone coffin lid fall on his head.

* There was Turkey Creek Johnson who was shot in the foot.

* There was the clerk behind the jewelry counter who was shot in the cheek.

* There was Cemetery Sam who accidentally shot himself in the hand after shooting the jewelry store clerk. "Just two dollars!" he screamed, for all that work! It was just too much for him so he went nutso-crazy. Poor guy.

And finally, there was Lord Jacob the Third, the corpse: he got stepped on, dropped, and drug through the dirt. Sorry, Jacob.

Well, hope you enjoyed these stories. And if you did, go buy Book Four: Murphy's Mad Monster Murder Mysteries. But don't pay too much for it, it's not that good…well, unless you like weird monster mystery stories, and I bet you do!

—The previous stories were written by Donald Kirk on Jan 25 and 26, 1964.

Murphy's Mad Monster Murder Mysteries

By Donald Kirk

CONTENTS

The following short stories are about strange occurrences caused by a certain book. The book, as you shall see, was appropriately named...

MURPHY'S MAD MONSTER
MURDER MYSTERIES

It was written by Murphy, a man whose location is still unknown (maybe he never really existed). Anyway, you'll find out why this book is unusual as you read the following unbelievable tales.

Now please turn the page...

1. THE TRANSIT EYE

"Look, Major," said a young man as he handed Murphy's Mysteries to a much older man. "I started reading a good mystery story written by this 'Murphy' fellow. It's quite a fascinating book. Murphy explained in his story how the invention was made. He even provided a blueprint that folded out of the book."

"What's the invention, Mario?" asked the Major.

"The Transit Eye."

"The Transit…Eye?"

"Yeah. Here look for yourself. With this invention, the man in the story could take any object, separate its molecules, send it for many miles through the air, and then re-combine the molecules to reconstruct the object in perfect condition."

"And the book," asked the Major, "actually explains how to make it?"

"Yes, except for one thing: the RAY, used in this invention, doesn't actually exist."

"I won't let that stop me."

"What do you mean?"

"The thing will exist when I finish building this TRANSIT EYE," pronounced the Major with a cunning smile.

"You can't build the Transit Eye," insisted Mario. "Why, you don't even have the equipment, and maybe this blueprint has no meaning. It's just part of a fictional story, you know."

"Fictional? You sure? Well, the only way to find out is to build it!"

Several days passed and in the front room of the Major's house were several stacks of wooden crates and corrugated cardboard boxes from various electronics manufacturers. Then the front doorbell rang. Mario, who was there, opened the door.

"A package for Major Mallory," announced the mailman standing outside the door. "Sign here, please."

Mario quickly signed for the package and closed the door. "This is the last of the equipment, Major. Now you can start building your vision of the Transit Eye."

Tick-tock, tick-tock, tick-tock, the Major worked day and night, around the clock, on his TRANSIT EYE, *tick-tock, tick-tock, tick-tock*, and at the end of the week it was finally finished, well except for the fact there was no RAY because it apparently didn't exist.

Mario quickly spoke, "I see you have the EYE finished, but where is that RAY you're going to use?"

"Here, before I show you the RAY, I'll show you how I...here, I'll show you. Look here in Murphy's book. The book is over uh, there, uh, now where did I put that book?"

"Major, I think you better get some sleep before you tell me. You haven't slept all week."

"Well, I think that's a...a good idea. I, I, I am tired. You CAN be sure of that."

Six hours later, the Major woke up and started explaining to Mario his plan for the RAY:

"I see you've found the book," said the Major. "Here, look at the footnote at the bottom of the page, there, below the diagram. You see it reads 'RAY: Y-A-R-E-H-T.'"

"Yes, I see it."

"Okay. Now, in the diagram of the Transit Eye the parts are lettered. Each of the letters Y-A-R-E-H-T are on certain parts in the diagram, that is, except for the letter 'E'! There is no letter 'E'. I think all the parts, if put together in the proper order, will produce the RAY."

"But, Major, where is the 'E' part?" asked Mario.

"Oh, well I believe that 'E' stands for 'Electricity'," replied the Major as his excitement soared. "All I have to do to finally get the invention to work is to plug in this cord."

"Plug it in then, I want to see it work," cried Mario.

The Major took the two halves of the invention and set them several feet apart. He then took a slice of pecan pie on a porcelain plate and put it in a compartment in one of the two halves. He closed the door to the compartment and then turned several dials and switches. The machine began to *whir,* and then *hum*, and then *buzz*, like a big hive of bumble bees. The sound was so very frightening.

All of a sudden, a ray of weird-colored light left one half of the invention and shot through the air to the other half. The second half also had a closed compartment so Mario opened it, and inside, was the slice of pecan pie on the plate completely reconstructed! Pie AND porcelain plate!

"It worked!" yelled Mario with a loud exciting enthusiasm. "The pie moved from one part of the invention to the other…invisibly! Just a ray of colored light, awesome, wow!"

"I told you I could do it," screamed the Major, "but now we've got to test it for a longer distance. And there can be nothing standing in between the two halves of the invention. We'll take the contraption out to the big farm field north of town."

The two excited men took the invention—and a gasoline-operated generator—to the big field. They set the two halves about a half-mile apart facing each other in a straight line, with no obstructions in between: no houses, no trees, no corn stalks—a clear line of sight.

The Major then put a big brown rat in the first compartment, closed the door, and turned the machine on. It *whirred* and *hummed* and *buzzed*. The molecules of the rat were separated and the strange light RAY sent the rat on its way through the air. But at that moment, a farmer walked in between the machines and stepped in front of the RAY. The RAY actually hit him!

There was a blinding white flash of light.

And at the same time, the sending half of the invention exploded and the Major standing next to it was…

After the flash of light died down, a monstrous, awful looking creature walked away from it. And wouldn't you know it, the monster was half rat and half man! It was either a very hairy man with a very long snout and little beady red eyes, or it was a big rat with little pink ears and human feet. The molecules of the rat must have mixed with the molecules of the human! There now appeared to be a new creature on planet Earth…a Ratman! This new Ratman, with its huge tail trailing behind it, scurried into the woods.

Meanwhile, at the receiving machine, Mario

was wondering what had happened. No rat appeared. Mario must have not heard the explosion. He decided to return to the transmitting part of the invention to see what was wrong. When he arrived at the sending half—that is, what little was left of it—and saw the dead Major, he was not really surprised. Why? He said to himself: I guess I should have told him what Murphy's story was really about, then maybe, he would not have built this horrible transit machine. The Major died just as the inventor did in the story. He is dead now, and it's my fault. In the story, a monster was created from two different creatures fused together. It must have happened here too. Oh, I haven't finished reading Murphy's book! I better find out what is going to happen next here in the real world.

Mario headed for the Major's house.

When he got there, he sat down in a chair and began to read Murphy's mystery book. But he read for only about five minutes and then fell asleep.

But only a short time passed.

Mario awoke and slowly opened his eyes. He saw something through a blurred vision, rubbed his eyes, and then cried out a wild, loud, curdling scream...

He saw the giant Ratman with long hair, tail, and all, looking squarely at him!

Mario suddenly jumped out of his seat, but he and the chair fell backward. The Ratman grabbed him and pulled him up as the creature's tail wrapped itself tightly around Mario. He shrieked another curdling fearful scream! The creature grabbed Mario around the neck with its long pointed claws. And it showed its long, sharp, ivory teeth. Mario yelled for help, but it was only in vain for no one heard him. The monster squeezed all the life out of him.

THE END

I wonder if this story ended the same way the story in the book ended? You know which book: MURPHY'S MAD MONSTER MURDER MYSTERIES.

Do you think it did? I wonder what happened to the Ratman? Do you know? Could he still be roaming the countryside?

It seems you've managed to get through one strange Murphy story, so now you can read the next eye-widening one. Do you dare? Then read on...

2. DISSOLVING GOO

A janitor was walking down a narrow hallway in an office building. He stopped in front of a door and unlocked it with one key hanging on a large ring of keys. He then went into a utility room full of brooms, mobs, and cans of floor wax. But, instead of working, the janitor pulled out a book hidden on a shelf, sat down in a cushioned chair, and began to read it. He thought to himself: I hope I can finish this book before the manager finds out that I've been reading during working hours...but I must finish; I have just thirteen more pages to go!

Twenty minutes later, the janitor finished reading the book, closed it, and said out loud, "That was a great surprise ending. The best book I've ever read!" Looking at the cover, the janitor said to himself, "It was written by this Murphy fellow. Some characters where, uh... I'm fall-ing a-sleeep..."

"The janitor yawned and slouched down in his chair. He had clearly, quietly, fallen soundly asleep.

Suddenly, the door creaked open and a large man walked in: IT WAS THE MANAGER! "Wake up you lazy, no good bum," yelled the manager with threatening, trembling eyeballs.

The janitor jumped up, knocked over his chair, and his book hit the floor.

"I see you've been reading again," barked the manager.

The manager grabbed Murphy's book off

the floor and threw it into the nearby furnace. The book quickly burst into yellow flames, not like the slow smoldering a closed book would normally do.

"Get back to work you lazy loafer! I ought to fire you, but I need you, so get back to work! This building is a dirty mess."

The manager pushed the janitor out the door and then locked the utility-room door behind him.

But meanwhile, something was happening in the furnace, something out of the ordinary, something very unusual, something extraordinary:

A slimy green goo began to seep out of the furnace door. It dripped out and flowed along the floor, slowly spreading, and spreading, and spreading…it seemed to be growing in size!

What was it?

Soon it completely covered the floor of the utility room. The strange, pulsating goo was beginning to seep under the locked door.

The janitor soon returned, took out his keys, and opened the door, but as he did, he slipped and fell into the goo. He screamed as the bubbling green liquid flowed over him.

What was this scary advancing stuff?

In no time, the janitor was completely covered by the weird pulsing yuck, and after only

a few minutes, the stuff had completely dissolved the janitor in to itself.

What do you think this goo was?

Does it FEED on humans?

The liquid was now spreading through the
halls...slowly expanding, and moving, and cov-
ering everything. OH NO! A man was coming
down the hall, getting closer, and closer, and
closer. He slipped on the green goo. The jelly-
like liquid enveloped him easily.

Dissolved, eaten, the helpless man!

It looked as if there was no limit to how
great an area the goo could cover. It continued
to seep into the nearby offices. Several men
rushed out of one of the rooms.

"Call the fire department," yelled one of the
men.

"Get the science bureau," yelled another.

"I'll get everyone out of the building...*ahhh-
hhh*...HEEELP!" A young lady slipped. A man
tried to pick her up and pull her away from the
deadly goo, but he also fell.

"Here's a rope," yelled another man as he
threw it to the victims trapped in the goo.

The woman was successfully pulled out,
but the man was horribly dissolved, only his
leather shoes still visible, floating quietly in the
yucky goo.

An hour later, everyone, still alive, was out

of the building except for three scientists wearing plastic protective suits. They were trying to examine the growing green gob of goo. All of the windows and doors, except for the front door, had been locked and the space at the bottom blocked with blankets before they arrived.

"This substance is not spreading as fast as it did at first," observed one of the scientists. "It's been nearly an hour since anyone was devoured by this yuck. Maybe it has to eat humans to grow."

"Maybe so, but we have to stop it somehow."

"Yes, we'll have to try different ways," said one scientist. "Miller, you go after a flame thrower, and Michael, you go see what else you can find that might kill this gooey green gob of goo."

A few minutes later, Michael returned carrying a dry-chemical fire extinguisher.

"While you were gone, Mike, the green goo shrank backward several yards along its perimeter and is actually decreasing in size."

"Great! Maybe it IS dying out from the lack of food."

"I sure hope so…oh, here, Miller is coming back."

Miller walked up to them and said, "The flame thrower will be here any minute now, but a large crowd is gathering outside and the press is trying to get in."

"This awful goo, if they only saw what it did, they wouldn't try to get in. But we can't tell them what's happening; it would start a panic. Anyway, this green stuff is shrinking so I don't think we should do anything to it now. We might actually do something that could cause it to grow again."

Meanwhile, at the back of the building, someone was breaking through a window: an obsessed news reporter was climbing through the small window wanting to get the story first, but, oh, instead, he slipped on the slimy green floor and fell into the gooey creature.

Within minutes, the reporter was completely dissolved, even his shoes disappeared!

"Hey!" called out Michael, "It's growing again. What happened? Get the flame thrower!"

Miller lit the flame thrower, squeezed the trigger, and a huge orange flame—like a dragon's bad breath—shot out onto the goo. The gushing green goo bubbled up, made a sizzling sound, and began to smoke.

The liquid then began to burn through the surrounding walls like an acid. Miller backed away and turned off the flame thrower.

And without warning, the jelly-like goo exploded, splattering all over the walls and onto the scientists. The walls of the office building collapsed, falling inward. The onlookers scrambled for their dear lives! Finally, after a long, threatening time, the building quit groaning and became very quiet.

The next day, after the building had burned to the ground and the ashes cooled, the remains of the building were examined. There was no sign of the victims except for a few bones, fingers, toes, and a few pairs of shoes. And there was no sign of the green gob of goo, BUT, there WAS an unburned object lying on the concrete slab among the smoldering ashes: a book bearing the name: MURPHY'S MAD MONSTER MURDER MYSTERIES!

THE END

3. THE PECAN PICKERS

A car was driving up a dirt road toward a white farmhouse with a front porch. The house was sitting among many large, old pecan trees. The car drove up to the house, stopped, and a tall man, and a very short man, got out. When I say very short, I mean very, very short. This man was no taller than two feet from head to toe! Just twenty-four inches tall! And he wasn't a little kid, he was smaller than that, and he was quite old looking, probably in his seventies. The two men walked to the back door and knocked on the screen door. It was soon opened by the owner, Mr. McBiddle. The short tiny man was the first to speak:

"We're pecan pickers, here to do a day's work for a day's pay."

"Okay, good, we need all the pickers we can muster. The pecans are plentiful," said the farmer. "You'll find burlap sacks inside that shed. When you finish your picking, bring your sacks back here and I'll weigh them on this scale. I'm paying eight cents a pound. Is that okay with you?"

"Yes sir, that will be fine," replied the tall, skinny man.

"Okay then, have at it."

The tall man and the little-biddy man headed for the shed. After the two strange men were out of sight of the farmer, the tall man picked up the little man and put him in his big, baggy, coat pocket. Yeah, that's right, that's how small he was!

A little while later, out in the pecan grove, the two funny-looking men were picking pecans off the ground and putting then in their sacks with incredible speed. They were moving so fast that they were just a blur to the human eye.

But before long, they began to slow down, moving slower and slower. And the men were actually throwing some of the pecans back onto the ground! I guess they didn't want to take any of the old, rotten ones. I guess.

That evening the two men came back to the shed with four large sacks of pecans.

"Well," said Mr. McBiddle as he weighed the last sack, "you've got four-hundred-seventy-eight pounds, the most I've ever seen two men pick up in one short afternoon. It's downright amazing!"

"As you said, there were, in deed, lots of pecans on the ground," replied the little man.

"Well, 478 times 8 is three thousand eight hundred twenty four pennies. That comes to 38 dollars and 24 cents. A tidy sum," said Mr. Mc-Biddle, quickly multiplying the numbers in his head. The farmer got his pocketbook and paid the men, but thankfully not in pennies. The two men climbed into their car and drove off, waving 'goodbye' on the way out. Nice men.

During the next few days, many other people came to pick pecans. Some stayed for only a few hours, others stayed all day.

But then, early one morning, a large box truck drove up to the farmhouse, but the driver wasn't here to pick pecans. He got out of his truck, walked around to the farmer's back door, climbed a few steps, and knocked.

After a long moment, the paneled door was opened, then the screen door, and the driver entered the house.

"I'm here to pick up your pecans. How many sacks do you have?"

"Fifty two sacks ready to go," replied Mr. McBiddle.

Two large men jumped out of the back of the truck and began to load pecans.

At this point in our story, a police car came up the gravel driveway. It stopped behind the truck, and a policeman in a blue uniform, and a woman who looked very worried, got out.

"Where's the owner of this pecan grove?" asked the policeman.

"In the house," replied the truck driver.

Mr. McBiddle came to the screen door.

"I'm from the missing persons bureau," said the policeman. "I, of course, am looking for a missing person."

The woman added, "And I know he was here yesterday. He's my son, and he said he was coming to your pecan grove."

"Yes, he might have been here picking pecans," replied the farmer. "We've had many pecan pickers. What does your son look like?"

"He's twelve years old with long, blond hair, and was wearing a baseball cap."

"Oh yes, I remember him. He came about ten o-clock yesterday morning, and he left about, oh…well, uh, gee, I don't remember him ever leaving. Hum? I know I never weighed his pecans!"

"Well, sir," interrupted the policeman, "we'll have to search the grove for him."

"By my guest, I'll walk with you. You can pick a few pecans. Can I get you a burlap sack?"

"Is that necessary?"

"No, not really."

So, Mr. McBiddle, the policeman, and the missing boy's mother, walked into the pecan grove without burlap bags.

Meanwhile, the trucker continued to load the sacks of pecans and leaves.

But just fifteen minutes later, the search party found the body of the missing boy. He was lying in the leaves, dead! A half-empty sack of pecans lay beside him. The policeman noticed a shelled pecan in his hand, and a half-chewed pecan in his mouth!

After a doctor had examined the body of the boy, he determined the cause of death to be an unknown form of poison! The doctor said he had never come across this toxin before.

A week passed, and another person in another part of the county died of the same mysterious poison. Strange, very strange.

"You know," said Mr. McBiddle to another picker, "I think that poison is coming from our pecans."

"But how could that be?"

"I don't know; it's just an idea. I'm going to tell the doctor about it tomorrow."

But by now, all the pecans that were picked up by the truck a week ago, had been delivered throughout the United States to be used in pecan pie, pecan butter, pecan cookies, and even ice-cream sundaes. I scream, you scream for... IS THIS COUNTRY DOOMED? ARE THE CITIZENS DOOMED? OR IS THE POISON THEORY ALL WRONG? Read on dear reader, or stop for a drink of water, and then press on.

In a nearby house, in a nearby town, in a nearby county, two men were laughing very hard as they read the headlines of the newspaper. It read: FOUR MEN NOW DEAD FROM UNKNOWN POISON!

"This is the best laugh I've had in years," chuckled a teeny-weeny little man, "and I owe it all to this book I borrowed from the public library: MURPHY'S MAD MONSTER MURDER MYSTERIES!"

During the next two weeks, three other people died of the same mysterious poison. But after that, there were no more deaths.

You ask why?

It's because the pecan grove farmer quit selling his pecan crop. Not all, but some of the pecans contained poison. You, of course, know who put the poison in the pecans: two strange pecan pickers—one tall, the other tiny—from another world who just wanted a laugh by playing a practical joke on the earthlings. An evil joke it was.

THE END

Don't stop reading just because you finished reading a nutty story. Take a short break, and then continue to read the next strange tale of weirdness…

4. INKY BUSINESS

This tale took place in a book-printing shop. It was like any other printing shop, that is, until it published a book entitled "Murphy's Mad Monster Murder Mysteries." The company was printing and selling quite a few copies. Bookstores and libraries all over the country were buying them like hotcakes. There was something about this book that attracted readers! It even attracted janitors and inventors and strange tall and tiny people. Anyway, this is what happened at the print shop:

"Yeah, Chief, that's right, we need more black ink. We just ain't got no more."

"Okay, a call to the Ink Corporation in Inksdale; they'll send us some more cans within a week."

"Okay, Chief." The press operator left the chief's office and went to the storeroom where he was going to get some ink solvent, rags, and a scrub brush. He figured he might as well clean the printing presses while they were sitting idle. He unlocked the storeroom door, walked in, and saw, over in the corner of the room, the empty ink cans.

"I better make double sure all these cans are empty before I return them to the Ink Company."

The press operator began to look in each can, and low-and-behold, there was one can still full of ink.

"I must have missed this one," the operator pointed out. He went to the main office and told the chief that there was no hurry in calling because there was still a whole can of black ink.

The next morning, the printing presses were again in full operation. The product was a mystery book. But before the book could be bound together with hard covers, it was checked for missing, torn, or blank pages.

But it was not long before the man who did the book inspecting, became furious. For the last hour, every single book he looked at, had something wrong with it. For example, every page in one book was blank, every page! And some books had type that was in many different colors even though the ink in the presses was only black! Some type was blurred, and some type was either very light grey or so dark and thick that it didn't dry, and that smeared the neighboring page. Oooh, what a big mess and a colossal waste of paper!

After the book inspector told the chief of this horrible, unexplained mishap, the printing presses were stopped, the press rollers examined, the black ink examined.

"Can't find nuttin' wrong with these here machines, Chief," said the press operator. "And there ain't nuttin' wrong with the black ink neither. No surprise there; what could be wrong with ink? Ink is ink, ain't it boss?"

"We'll start the presses again tomorrow and see what happens."

"Okay, chief. See you tomorrow."

The next day, the operator re-inked the press rollers, put on new rolls of paper and started the presses. They geared up to full speed and paper rolled smoothly over the ink rollers and over the impression plates. Off the press came the first large sheets each containing several book-sized pages before they could be cut to the required book size.

"Hum, looks okay to me. Why it looks perfect. Sharp, clear, clean…dry type." The operator then ran his fingers over the paper… *aaaaah*, it's hot, the paper's hot as fresh campfire ashes! It actually burned my fingers."

The chief ran up to the operator, "What to blazes happened?'

"This ink is sizzling hot!"

"Where is the new sheet?"

"I dropped it on the floor," answered the frightened operator.

And just as the chief reached down to pick it up, it burst into flames and quickly burned to ashes.

"Boy, it must have been really hot," declared the operator.

"Yeah, hot as a deep, red fire, and that's hot!"

The next day, again checking the printed words for dryness, the press operator touched the next run of sheets and found they had turned to acid! He screamed, "*Aaaaaaaah!*" as the skin melted off his finger tips!" *Oooough…*

An ambulance raced to the rescue. The book inspector, press operator, and the other workers at the book-making company, quickly decided to quit their jobs.

"It ain't safe 'round chere no more!"

"I'm firing myself from this here job!" yelled the foreman as he walked out.

In a matter of just a short while, everyone had quit or fired himself. The only person left was the chief. With no workers to help him, he would go out of business. And what's more, the moveable metal type in the printing press was ruined by the ACIDIC black ink! And where ever a drop of black ink had dripped on the floor, there was a big hole…all the way through the concrete and into the ground!

As the chief looked at the now silent presses and the darkened printing shop, he said to himself: That INK did it! That INK ruined me! I'll never use ink again, never, never, never! The chief picked up the remaining can of black ink and poured it onto the floor. What happened now was unbelievable!

Some ink turned yellow, some turned blue and green, and some turned bright red. Then some of the ink began to burn and smoke. And some ink just disappeared! Yeah, disappeared. Well, just everything imaginable happened. Some drops of ink exploded like a firecracker and splatters of the ink hit the ceiling rafters and that caused the roof of the building to cave in. The walls fell inward and the concrete floor crumbled! The chief fell into a deep crater and was never to be seen again...and that's how the story ends. Bye!

THE END

Many more incidents occurred because of the unusual book titled MURPHY'S MAD MONSTER MURDER MYSTERIES, but because of the lack of time and space, I have told you of only a few of the mysterious, unexplained occurrences associated with this book. If you know of any other weird stories that happened when someone read Murphy's book, please write me. I hope you have enjoyed these frightening tales and so now you can throw this book away...or I dare you to give it to a friend. He, he! Ha, ha!

—Written by Donald Kirk on April 23 through April 25, 1964.

SCARY ADVENTURE STORIES FOR BOYS

Mr. Graves and the Suitcase Murders (a.k.a. The Evil Gadget Man)

By Donald Kirk

CONTENTS
Mr. Graves and The Suitcase Murders

This story is about a sinister man with a diabolical plot to create ghastly headlines in the newspapers around the country. His wicked ways resulted in many horrifying deaths.

Turn the page to find out how he did it…

MR. GRAVES
AND THE SUITCASE MURDERS

CHAPTER ONE

Our story begins in Queen City, California.

"Ha-ha-ha, this will do the trick," said a tall, skinny man as he removed a cork from a long test tube. From the test tube, the man poured a bubbling red liquid into a large anthill. The hill of ants quickly began to bubble up with steam rising from the hole. Ants scooted out and dashed in all directions. The tall man jumped back, got into his car, and drove off. He made his way to a train station where he parked his car and took a large, alligator-skin suitcase out of the trunk.

"A one-way ticket to Dry Hills, Nevada, please, sir."

"The train leaves in fifteen minutes, Mr. Graves."

"Good."

Meanwhile, something strange was happening just outside of town:

"Come here mother, in the north pasture, down by the pond."

"What is it, dear?"

Just then something huge and very strange-looking came up behind the boy's mother.

"Look Mom! Behind You! Run for your life!" A giant..."

"*Aaaaahhhhhhhh*, he's got me! Help me, Johnny. *Aaaah!*"

"Run for help, Johnny, go get help!"

Johnny ran for town, but the big-headed creature with two large antennae and six hairy legs came chasing after him.

A pedestrian turned to see the awful creature coming up behind him.

"Look! We're being invaded by giant insects, monster-sized ants!" The pedestrian ran into the nearby General Store. "Help, look what's outside in the street!"

"What did you say, Mister? *Aaaaahhhhhhhhh...*"

Everyone in the store ran and hid behind the counter. A giant ant crashed through the huge plate glass window. Shards of glass flew everywhere. The ant's giant mandibles opened wide when it stuck its head in the open window. It's long flopping antennae swung around searching for signs of anything moving.

A customer got up and ran in panic, "*Aaaaahhhhhhhh!*" But he was quickly picked up by the ant's huge claw-like mandibles and was swung around, and around, and around. The creature banged the customer's body against the wall until his body was finally released and fell to the floor. But his HEAD remained stuck in the ant's claws!

"Eeerro, Eeeerro," came a loud piercing shriek that was suddenly heard along the city streets. It was the city's evacuation siren! And shrieks of fear were heard all over town as people ran in every direction like ants would on a stepped-on anthill. Hundreds of huge, awful-looking ants crawled through the streets picking up people, crushing them with their mandibles, and then stinging them with the giant stinger on their abdomen. The critters then sucked the life-sustaining juices from the humans. In just a matter of a few minutes, cars and people, and cats and dogs, had crowded the streets trying to leave the city.

Meanwhile, Mr. Graves was riding safely on a passenger train headed for Nevada. He picked up his alligator-skin suitcase, set it on the seat, and opened it. The suitcase was divided into small compartments for holding bottles of colored liquids along with various mechanical and electrical gadgets. Also in the suitcase was a small black briefcase. In it, Mr. Graves took out a small tin box and on the outside of the box was a small yellow knob with numbers on it. Graves also had a railroad map and a timetable in his possession. After several minutes of study, and messing with a calculator, Mr. Graves set the knob on the tin box to "twenty minutes."

A few minutes later, the train came to a stop at a small railroad station in Dry Hills, Nevada. Mr. Graves got off the train with his big suitcase, BUT he left behind the tin box, having placed it under his seat on the train...on purpose.

WHAT WILL HAPPEN NOW?

After new passengers boarded the train, it steamed out of the station.

Mr. Graves took a look at his pocket watch as the train began its climb up a long grade into the hills. What's going to happen now? Keep reading to find out...

CHAPTER TWO

A couple of minutes later, there was a huge explosion in the hills! Passenger cars and people were thrown violently into the air!

Mr. Graves smiled and turned away as railroad workers ran up the track to find out what had happened. Graves flagged a taxicab that took him to the *Sleepless Nites Hotel*, the only hotel in town. So he stayed there.

The next morning Mr. Graves bought a newspaper. It had two unusual headlines: GIANT 30-FOOT-TALL ANTS RUN RAMPANT THROUGH QUEEN CITY! PASSENGER TRAIN EXPLODES OUTSIDE OF DRY HILLS. SEVEN DEAD, THIRTEEN INJURED! Graves smiled at these headlines.

After breakfast, Mr. Graves went for a walk. He casually walked down the railroad track in the direction he had come carrying his small black briefcase. It wasn't long before he came to an automatic block signal. The signal was now red, which meant that any train approaching had to stop. It was red because the track ahead was still blocked from the wrecked train the evening before. Graves climbed up on the block signal with a small wrench he had taken out of his briefcase. He then unscrewed a few nuts and attached a copper wire. The signal light then turned green! Oh no, there will be big trouble now!

Back at the hotel, Mr. Graves packed his suitcase. He now had plans to leave town on a BUS. Of course, he had no desire to take the train! He took a bottle of green fluid from his suitcase, put it in his coat pocket, checked out of the hotel, and found his way to the mechanical room. Inside the room sat the air-conditioner with air-intake vents. Graves put on a gas mask and stood in front of the vents. He opened the bottle and a green, swirling vapor was released into the air. The vapor was quickly sucked into the air-conditioner vents. The vapor, in just a few minutes, will have circulated throughout the hotel! Mr. Graves hurried out of the hotel and hopped on the bus to Kansas.

The next day, after a very long bus ride, Mr. Graves arrived in a small town in Kansas called "Plainsview." Again he bought a newspaper. On the front page, there were more tragic headlines: TRAIN COLLIDES WITH DERAILED TRAIN OUTSIDE OF DRY HILLS, NEVADA! MANY PASSENGERS HURT! POISONOUS GAS IN HOTEL MAKES EACH GUEST SICK AS A DOG! These headlines are not surprising to Graves. (I wonder why!)

After reading every word of the dreadful stories, Mr. Graves thumbed a ride to an old farmhouse a few miles east of Plainsview. Now, why could he be going there?

CHAPTER THREE

The yard around the farmhouse had grown up in weeds. White paint was peeling off the wood siding and there were massive spider webs all over the front porch. Mr. Graves climbed into the house through a broken-out window. The inside of the house was as run-down as the outside and tables and chairs were overturned. A thick layer of dust covered the wooden floors. Mr. Graves walked over to a wall where he then pulled out a loose board. Behind the board was a metal box with wires running from it and back into the wall cavity. There were two buttons on the box. Graves immediately pushed one of them.

The floor made a creaking sound and then a wooden trapdoor on hinges opened in the floor.

Mr. Graves pushed the other button.

A light went on down stairs in a concrete-lined basement. Mr. Graves walked down the steep basement stairs—thirteen narrow steps—and when he reached the bottom, he pushed another button.

The trap door in the floor above him closed.

The basement, it turned out, was full of scientific laboratory equipment: oscilloscopes, scales, glass flasks, metal cutting tools, and so on, and so forth.

This house happened to be where Mr. Graves's grew up, and many years ago, he had this concrete bunker built secretly. He was now using it as a laboratory for making his wicked solutions and sinister gadgets.

Mr. Graves took off his coat and started to work on something. After several hours of hard work making chemicals and building little electrical devices, Graves had finally finished his latest diabolical project. He opened his suitcase and put a small wooden box into his gadget-filled suitcase, but as he did so, some black powder fell out of the box. Mr. Graves put several more glass bottles of his special concoctions into his suitcase. One bottle contained a familiar red liquid and the other a foaming green substance. He replaced his already-dirty clothing on top of the gadgets to hide them.

"I'm going to have to get these clothes washed soon," he said to himself. Graves closed the large suitcase, climbed the stairs out of the concrete bunker, closed the trap door, and left the farmhouse through the broken glass window. He hitched a ride back to town and went to a Chinese laundry.

"I can have your clothes done right away, Mr. Graves."

"Okay, I'll be back in an hour, Ling Lee, but please hurry. I have to catch a plane."

"Yes, Mr. Graves."

Graves went to the nearby popcorn plant that made *Whizbang-Pop* and snuck in the backdoor. He went to the huge vat of canola oil and poured a bottle of green foam into the hot bubbling oil. He then left the plant and returned to town.

When Mr. Graves returned to the laundry, Ling Lee had finished cleaning and pressing Graves' clothes.

"Here, Mr. Graves, that will be eighty-five cents."

"Hey wait," hollered Mr. Graves, "My white pants have a hole burnt in them!"

"I'm sorry, sir, but when I pressed your pants, I ironed over what was gunpowder, I think, in your pants pocket! It exploded and made a big hole…"

"But, didn't you wash the pants?"

"No, sir, you give me clean pair of pants. I see no need, they were just wrinkled, so I…"

"I have got to go. Here's your eighty-five cents."

Mr. Graves walked out just in time to get to a small airport and catch a prop plane to Ohio. The plane soon reached the Ohio border and Graves landed at the International Airport in Aileron.

I wonder what he has up his sleeve—or in his pocket—this time? Is it deadly or destructive? Keep reading to find out.

CHAPTER FOUR

Mr. Graves climbed the winding stairs that led to the airport control tower. He then climbed a ladder to the roof of the control tower and he had his suitcase with him! Mr. Graves laid it down on the tin roof, opened it, took out several electronic devices, and a Phillips screwdriver. He screwed together a box-like contraption. There was a metal loop at the top and several dials on the side. He flipped a switch and the loop started turning.

What is this thing? What is he going to do?

Mr. Graves took out what looked like a bird, but it was made of tin! A mechanical bird with aluminum folding wings. He put the robotic bird down on the roof and flipped a switch on a small black box. The bird's eyes glowed red.

"Powered up and ready," said Mr. Graves gleefully as he closed his gadget-filled suitcase, left the box and the bird on the roof, and climbed back down the ladder and tower stairs. He quickly took a city taxi to a hotel.

The next morning, Mr. Graves went for coffee and the morning newspaper. It was a special edition that read: TWO PLANES COLLIDE IN MID-AIR OVER THE AILERON AIR-

PORT. PRIVATE PLANE CRASHES ONTO RUNWAY! It slid into a parked jetliner that was fueling up and exploded! The police are trying to track down the cause of radio interference that prevented the tower from communicating with landing aircraft.

We know what caused the interference don't we? It was Mr. Graves's box on the roof: a radio transmitter jamming the traffic-control signals. But what was the mechanical bird for?

Read the next chapter to find out...

CHAPTER FIVE

The bird was a radio-controlled device that could fly around the runway until it was sucked into an airplane's jet engine, causing the plane to crash. How sinister was that! What was wrong with this evil man? Why did he hate people so much?

The entire airport was closed down until they could determine there to be no more flying robotic birds. Thousands of passengers couldn't get home and arriving planes were diverted to other airports, affecting air traffic all across the United States. All because of these mysterious metal birds!

Graves read another headline in the morning paper: GIANT ANTS STILL AT LARGE IN CALIFORNIA!

Mr. Graves laughed real hard and fell out of his chair. He turned the page on his newspaper, but quit laughing when he read this headline:

THE TRAIN WRECKS AT DRY HILLS ARE NO ACCIDENT! A tall, slender man in dark suit was seen tampering with block signal. Man reported to have taken bus to Plainsview, Kansas. Police are on an all-out search for him.

Mr. Graves threw the newspaper down and stuffed a change of clothes into his suitcase.

I think he's going to leave in a hurry. What do you think?

He left the hotel, but didn't take a bus, or a passenger train, or even an airplane. Instead, he hitched a ride in a railroad boxcar where he had the company of a hobo as he rode a freight train headed east toward New York. He offered the hobo a bottle of red liquid, telling him it was whiskey. OH NO!

A long night passed, but the next morning, just before dawn, Mr. Graves jumped out of the boxcar. But the hobo was no longer with him and the hobo didn't jump off the train. Instead, he had been thrown off! The Hobo was killed by the fall. But why did the evil Graves do it?

Mr. Graves found himself standing in a wet, slimy, swampy area with the dead hobo next to him. Graves left the hobo in the swamp and walked along the railroad track with his suitcase full of deadly things. It was not long before he arrived in a small farming village called "Pitchfork" somewhere in the state of New York. He then hopped a ride on a bus going west.

Meanwhile something was happening in Pitchfork:

"*Aaaaaaaahhhhhhhah! Heeeelllllllp!*" Someone was screaming!

What's happening now?

Stay tuned to find out…

CHAPTER SIX

A giant female mosquito, with huge, purple, multi-balled eyes, was chasing a man down the street. The mosquito knocked down the man and sucked bright red blood, sucking every last drop from his body. He was now dead! Other mosquitoes flew into town, buzzed over pickup trucks and landed on pedestrians, knocking them down. They stuck their two barbed hooks into the people to hold them down and then stuck their long, tubular snouts into their bellies…sucking joyfully until the humans shriveled up. It was an awful, sickening sight!

And the residents of Pitchfork still didn't know that a squadron of giant mosquitoes were flying toward their town! They had better get inside and lock their doors, right quick!

Meanwhile, back in Plainsview, Kansas, a lady bought a jar of *Wizbang-Pop* popcorn and took it home. She poured the corn into a pan and put it on the stove. She added a teaspoon full of the green canola oil that came with the *Wizbang-Pop*. She put the lid on, shook the pan for one minute, then two more minutes, then three. The popcorn finally started to pop and pop some more. After four minutes (that's 240 seconds), the lid began to bounce off the pan and white popcorn kernels started flowing out. Finally, the lid blew off, hitting the ceiling. The lady jumped back fearful, dropping the pan on the hot stove. Popcorn started popping into the air, shooting everywhere. Kernels whizzed by the frightened lady so she dove to the floor. The popcorn kept popping, harder, and harder, and harder. The blasting kernels actually hit the dining room windows and shattered them. Some of the kernels were so powerful, they shot through the sheetrock walls like lead bullets. The house was now peppered with holes and looked like a giant food strainer. The scared lady crawled to her telephone and called the police station.

"Yes ma'am."

"Help. I'm being hit with popcorn."

"You too, lady? People all over town are calling us! Did you try to pop the *Wizbang-Pop* brand?"

"Yes, yes, that's it, help meeeeee…"

"All we can suggest, Madam, is to get out of the house! *Wizbang-Pop* popcorn has gone crazy in Plainsview! It's terrorizing the town! Some houses are getting so many holes in them that they fall down! What a mess. All, it seems, caused by a green popcorn oil!

Elsewhere in town, two plain-clothes policemen were searching the town looking frantically for Mr. Graves. They checked with nearly every person in town to see if anyone had seen him. No such luck. They then walked into a Chinese laundry.

"Hello, we're looking for a tall, well-dressed, slender man, and he may be carrying a suitcase. Have you seen him?"

"Ah yes. I see him. He had gunpowder in his pants pocket."

"Gunpowder!"

"Yes, when I ironed his pants it blew a hole in his pants!"

"Did you get his name?"

"Oh sure, I know man. He live around here when he a boy."

"Exactly where?"

"On a farm just north of town."

"And his name?"

"Mr. Graves. He indeed a strange man."

"Well thanks, we'll head for the farmhouse now."

"Oh no, officer, he not there. He left on east-bound bus."

"Bus? Where to?"

"I don't know."

"Well, maybe we can find out at the bus station."

The two policemen left the Chinese laundry and drove to the bus station where the ticket teller told them Mr. Graves purchased a ticket to New York City. At that, the police took a plane to New York as quickly as they could.

CHAPTER SEVEN

In New York City, Mr. Graves entered a large Laundromat and laid his gadget-filled suitcase on top of one of the washing machines. He opened it, removed a cardboard box, put a quarter in the washer, and started it.

Cold water flowed swiftly into the washer. Mr. Graves then poured a white flaky powder into the washing machine. He started all the other washers and poured the white substance into them also. But he left the lids to all the washing machines open! He then closed his suitcase and walked out with it.

That's strange, I wonder what he's up to now!

Mr. Graves checked into a hotel on Time Square after buying a city newspaper. The headline read: MONSTROUS MOSQUITOES GRIP TOWN IN TERROR! And on the next page: POPCORN IN PLAINSVIEW PANIC PEOPLE! The sinister Graves smiled; he knew the *Wizbang-Pop* popcorn was being shipped all over the country! He-he!

Meanwhile, the two policemen from Plainview flew into New York. They contacted Police Headquarters and an all-points-bulletin was put out for the evil Mr. Graves.

Back in the Laundromat, large soapy bubbles were gushing out of the washing machines. The Laundromat was filling to the ceiling with bubbling soap bubbles! A gushing white gob of foam began to flow through the doors and out onto the street.

Back in the hotel on Time Square, Mr.

Graves was looking out the window with a pair of binoculars. There, coming down a side street, and flowing into the square, was a huge six-foot wall of foaming soap! Cars were overtaken by this white bubbling mass and started skidding around on the slimy-slick streets. Out-of-control vehicles crashed into each other. Thousands of cars were becoming one big auto scrap yard! People climbed out of their cars trying to escape the attacking foam that filled the Square. But they too slipped on the soap scum and slid and fell every which way. They could breath only soap bubbles that might suffocate them. Mr. Graves lowered his binoculars and smiled an evil grin of satisfaction.

Then there was a knock at the door. Mr. Graves tensed up. "Who could that be? I didn't order any room service," he said out loud.

"Mr. Graves, is that you?" came a voice in the hallway. Graves wasted no time climbing out the window onto an emergency fire-exit landing. The weight of his body automatically lowered the steel stairs. He hurried down the steps and found himself engulfed in the thick white foam.

Outside his room, a waiter said to himself, "I guess he's not in. I just wanted to give him his free hot dinner. Oh, well." The waiter turned and walked away.

Later that day, the fire department flooded Time Square with millions of gallons of water so they could dilute the soap and wash it into the river. It would take days to clean up the mess, but you can bet the cars and the streets of Time Square were now very clean!

The next day, the morning newspaper had another very large headline: THE SUITCASE MURDERER SLIPS ON SOAP SUDS AND BREAKS HIS ARMS AND LEGS. THE POLICE GIVE HIM A LIFE SENTENCE IN A GADGET FACTORY, but this headline, Mr. Graves will never get to read it!

THE END

Hope you enjoyed the story. The police eventually found that Mr. Graves was the cause of the following incidents—headlines:

* Giant Killer Ants Attack Queen City, California.

* Two Trains Wreck near Dry Hills, Nevada.

* Mechanical Bird and Radio Transmitter Cause Several Plane Crashes in Aileron, Ohio.

* *Wizbang-Pop* Factory Explodes When Worker Gets Popcorn Kernels In Canola Oil.

* Giant Sucking Mosquitoes Shrivel Up People in Pitchfork, New York.

* Huge Soap Bubbles Smother New York

City Residents. Auto Insurance Rates Go Up!

    * A Sinister Laboratory Found In Plainsview, Kansas. Police Believe Concrete Walls Used To Test Popcorn Formula!

    * A Suitcase With Sinister Gadgets Found In Hotel Room. Suitcase Lets Out Mysterious Gas When Opened, Causes Everyone In Hotel To Fall Asleep For a Week!

—Written by Donald on June 16th through June 18th, 1964.

SCARY ADVENTURE STORIES FOR BOYS

Mistress Mary's Mortal Magic Mischief
FOUR SCARY STORIES IN ONE

By Donald Kirk

CONTENTS

The following short stories are events that occurred because of a certain lady's bad behavior...MISTRESS MARY'S MORTAL MAGIC MISCHIEF.

Mistress Mary was a modern-day WITCH who would cast the oddest kind of spells...usually deadly ones! You will find out what I mean as you read the following gruesome tales.

Now turn the page...

MINGLED MISHMASH

Before we get to the gruesome stories, I want to tell you a little about Mistress Mary's concoctions because they were somewhat different than any other witch's brew. Mary made her creations in a special electronic pot with a dial control.

In every bit of her Mingled MishMash (brew) she used wort (various plants and herbs). Mary's exotic herbs seemed to be the thing that gave the brews their deadly spice! Mistress Mary also used a paste made of wheat flour that was dried in the form of slender tubes. I think a common name for it is *macaroni*! Many times Mary also used mushrooms of the Toadstool variety!

Mary not only used ingredients like this, but she liked to use spider goo and lady fingers. The ingredients, of course, depended on the intended use for the brew.

Now that I have told you something about Mistress Mary's Mingled Mishmash, you can begin to read the following horrifying stories...

1. MYOCARDIOGRAPH

"Scalpel."

"Scalpel."

"Scouring pads."

"Pads."

"Tweezers."

"Tweezers."

"Um, yes, here's the infected kidney, Doctor."

"Cotton."

"Cotton."

"His blood pressure is falling, Doctor."

"And his heart rate has slowed down considerably!"

"Give me the needle and catgut…quick!"

I can't stand the site of blood," cried Dr. Murphy Millblood, a doctor who joked even during the most serious moments.

"Doctor, his heart is pumping very slowly."

"You know what to do. He must have had a tired heart because removing a kidney is a routine operation…"

"Too late Doctor…he's departed this life."

It was two days later when an ambulance came racing up the back drive, jerked to a stop, and the back doors flew open. A badly injured man on a gurney was lifted out.

"Emergency! Get the operating room ready. This man has a badly fractured leg and broken ribs."

In the operating room a surgical team was hard at work:

"Boy, this man really messed himself up…"

"Car accident, sir," added one of Doc Mill-blood's assistants.

"He has more bones on the outside of his leg than inside…"

"And I'm afraid we're not going to be able to put them back in…"

"He missed a river bridge!"

"But he didn't miss a boat propeller."

"They'll call him funny bones…"

"We're going to have to amputate."

Sometime later, as they finished removing his leg, the doctor put down the bloody meat saw:

"His heart stopped, sir!"

"WHAT?"

"That's what the Myocardiograph* indi-cates…"

"Doc, it was no heart attack this time."

(*The Myocardiograph is an instrument for recording the movements of the heart muscle.)

Ten minutes later, after having had a cup of heavily caffeinated coffee, Dr. Millblood was called into the main office because the Chief of Surgery wanted to talk to him.

The Chief spoke: "Every patient you've operated on in the last few days has died."

"Three to be exact."

"Three, so what gives?"

"I don't know. Neither of them should have died. Ever since we got that new Myocardio…"

"I guess you know you're about to loose your medical license!"

The two men continued to talk until they were stopped by an emergency call for Dr. Millblood.

Thirteen minutes later, Dr. Millblood walked out of the operating room with his head down. As he removed his latex gloves, he mumbled to himself, "just a routine appendicitis…minor surgery."

An assistant rushed out of the operating room calling out, "Doctor, wait! You didn't kill the boy; something is wrong with the myocardiograph!"

"You mean he's not dead?" asked the doctor as he looked up.

"No, he's dead alright, but…"

"But what? What happened?"

Dr. Millblood talked to the assistant for a few minutes and then ran outside and picked up an alley cat. He brought the cat inside and took it to the operating room. Two assistants in the room hooked the myocardiograph to the cat. The three people sat down and closely watched the needle moving up and down on the recording instrument.

"Look, the cat's heart is slowing down—it was beating normal when we brought it in!"

A few minutes later, the cat's heart stopped pumping blood! In other words, the cat died!

"Just as you figured, doctor. The myocardiograph controls the heart it's hooked up to! It alone is stopping the beating hearts!"

"Who sold us that myocardiograph?" asked the doctor sternly.

"I don't know."

DOES THE READER KNOW?

IT COULDN'T BE MISTRESS MARY COULD IT?

THE END

2. MUCOUS MEMBRANE AND THE MEDIUM

"Come in Miss. Madam Margaret will be ready for you in just a minute."

A young brown-haired lady came through a large door and was taken into a small, spooky, dimly-lit room. The room was empty of all furniture except for a round table sitting in the middle of the room. The table was covered with geometric designs and strange-looking symbols.

"Sit here, please, Miss," directed the butler.

Presently, a large woman with long, black hair walked into the room. She was wearing a black gown with an animal-bone necklace around her neck. On the necklace was a large trinket. Madam Margaret sat down on the opposite side of the table.

"Give me your hands," she requested.

Their hands met in the center of the table.

"Now Miss, did you not say you wanted to contact your uncle?"

"Yes, I do want to contact the poor man. I hope he will tell me where his will is."

READ ON...

By now you may have realized that Madam Margaret was a medium—a person with supernatural powers who can communicate with the dead. And the young woman was a victim of this nonsense: she had paid two hundred dollars for this service. Anyway, the lights were turned off, but a hand full of candles were left burning. The medium soon made contact with the girl's uncle and the uncle actually came into view! But he was barely visible through a thick haze. After some talking, the uncle disappeared into nothingness, the lights were turned on, and the young woman left. The butler then came in from another room and spoke to the medium: "Another sucker, ha ha."

"And we're two-hundred dollars richer! Your deep voice and the layer of mirrors made it a cinch."

You might be wondering how the medium and the butler knew what a dead man looked like, and how they made a dead man's image appear in the small room. The truth is, they got a photograph of the dead person, and in a room above the small room where the medium was seated, the butler operated a projector that magnified the picture to life size. The image was then sent through a smoke box and reflected by mirrors to the first floor. As a result of the smoke machine, the ghost had a hazy appearance. The butler then talked through a speaker that distorted his voice.

Now back to the story.

It was now midnight, and there was a dark figure moving across a nearby graveyard. The figure walked to the center of the graveyard and raised its arms toward the stars. Out of the blue, a puff of white smoke spread out over the graveyard like thick fog as the mysterious figure walked away and disappeared into the smoke.

The next evening, Madam Margaret had an appointment with another lady. The lady was taken into the small room and the butler headed upstairs, but just as the butler reached the top of the stairs, he tripped and rolled head over heels down the stairs.

Meanwhile, the medium began her well-rehearsed performance.

"I want to speak to my blind father," spoke the victim.

Madam Margaret had the lady hold her hands, that is, after she had paid the two hundred dollars. The lights went out and the medium quickly contacted the dead father...but he did not come into view. You could only hear him speak. The lady and the dead father spoke to each other for a long time, connecting like long-lost friends.

Finally, when it was all over and the lady had left, Madam Margaret went through a secret door in a paneled wall and found the butler lying unconscious at the bottom of the stairway.

The Madam slapped the butler's face and he quickly regained consciousness.

"What happened?" asked Madam Margaret.

"I...I don't know, oh yes, I remember now, I fell down the stairs."

"Are you alright?"

"Yes, I think so," replied the butler.

"You sure did a good job of acting as the blind man's voice tonight..."

"But, I didn't..."

"How did you know where our victim was born and that other information you gave us?"

"No, wait, I never got to the upstairs room!"

"What?"

"I mean, I fell down the stairs and was knocked unconscious BEFORE, your performance. It couldn't have been MY voice you heard."

"Are you sure?"

"Yes."

"Have I really contacted the dead?"

"It seems so, Madam."

"Or someone else was upstairs, that must be what happened!"

The butler hurried upstairs to see if anyone was there. No one there! Not a living soul. He

Mistress Mary's Mortal Magic Mischief

then closed and locked the door to the projector room and returned to the first floor. "No Madam Margaret, no one was there, I'm sure of it!"

"I can't believe, I don't believe it!"

"Madam, maybe you could try to communicate with my mother. She died just two weeks ago."

"Yes, good idea, we can find out if I'm really a medium."

The butler and Madam Margaret walked into the small room, sat at the round table, held hands, turned out the lights, and attempted to contact the butler's mother. After some weird, perplexing gibberish, the room became very cold, so very icy cold.

"I've contacted her!" shouted the medium. "She's in this very room! You may speak to her."

"Hello mother, mother? I have missed you... so very much."

Immediately, a voice was heard in the darkness: "I bet you have."

"That's my mother! That's her voice!"

"And look over there in the haze, there she is!"

The hazy image of mother spoke again: "It's me you can be sure, your dear mother that was killed by you! How could you murder me for a little life insurance money? You're a bad son, very bad. I thought I raised you better. I'll get even with you!"

THE END

You might be interested to know that the butler got the electric chair because his conscious got the best of him and he turned himself in. And Madam Margaret was put in jail because her con game as a medium was, of course, illegal. And while in jail she went mad because no one would believe that she finally really could communicate with the dead! Do you believe she could? Can you explain this story? Mistress Mary maybe could!

You are probably wondering what the "Mucous Membrane" had to do with the story. Well, here's the answer: The mucous membrane is a thin layer of tissue in the nose and ear and mouth cavities of the body that communicate with the exterior world: the smelling, the hearing, and the speaking. In the middle of the story, Mistress Mary put a spell on the mucous membranes of the dead bodies laying in the graveyard. The spell gave these membranes the ability to receive and transmit signals, that is, to receive any voice addressed to it and to send the thoughts of the dead to the medium talking to them. Understand?

Well, if not, sleep on it, then read the next exciting story…

3. MILKWEEDS
AND MUSTARD GAS

"Just look! Melvin Mundy, look! Those milkweeds are beginning to take over the whole dad burn yard. Before long there won't be any grass left."

"Don't worry dear, I'll get rid of those weeds even if I have to do the work myself," declared Mr. Mundy.

"Of course, you'll do the work yourself; you're going to pull up every last one of those weeds…and you're starting this weekend!" ordered Mrs. Martha Mundy.

It was now Friday and Mr. Mundy had just come home from work.

"Martha, look what I've got," said Melvin as he held up a Mason jar with a yellowish liquid in it.

"What have you got?"

"A weed killer to spray on the milkweeds."

"Good for you. Now you've got something

to do. Get rid of those dad-blasted confounded weeds."

Melvin changed his clothes and went to work. He put the weed killer into a hand sprayer and began to spray the chemical all over the yard...for over an hour.

When Melvin came into the house that evening, he sat down to read the newspaper.

"Look here Martha, here on the front page: it says that a woman was out in her yard pulling weeds when she suddenly became sick and fell to the ground. And shortly afterword, her son found her lying in the yard. He took her to the hospital, her skin blistered all over...and they couldn't determine how!"

"Well, I declare, if that don't beat all...well come on dear, dinner's ready."

The weekend went by and Melvin finished spraying the front and backyard. On Monday, he went back to work. While Melvin was gone, Martha talked with herself: "that poison doesn't seem to be doing anything to those weeds, and if I know Melvin, he won't get on his hands and knees to pull those weeds."

"Who did you buy the weed killer from?" asked Martha when Melvin came home that evening. "It doesn't seem to be doing any good, the weeds are just growing taller."

Mistress Mary's Mortal Magic Mischief

"I got the weed killer from an old lady peddler selling goods on the street. She said it was one of her sure-fire potions. Guaranteed to kill those weeds, she said."

"She's a swindler. The weed killer doesn't work. Now you get out there and start pulling those weeds, every last one of them!"

"I'll do it this weekend. I've got office work to do now."

"Okay, but you do it THIS weekend, no more putting it off."

Melvin Mundy went back to work the next day and Martha decided to start pulling some of the weeds herself.

That evening, Melvin returned home:

"Martha, look, in today's paper: another victim of a mysterious sickness while pulling weeds...Martha! MARTHA! Where are you? I guess you're in the backyard."

Melvin went to the backyard and found Martha lying on the ground unconscious. Her skin was badly blistered. Melvin Mundy called for an ambulance.

Soon, both Mundy's were at the hospital:

"This is the third case. This sickness makes no since,'" said Doctor Mold. All I know is what the patients have told me. They say they fell sick only minutes after they began pulling milkweeds. And they all had recently sprayed the weeds with a poison. And they said they got the weed killer from an old lady peddler."

Just then, a nurse walked in. "Doctor, the first victim of this illness has just died!"

"Oh no!" cried Melvin Mundy. "My wife, she'll be next!"

"The police are trying to track down the peddler," said the nurse.

"I think the weed killer is poisonous when breathed," added the doctor.

Another doctor rushed into the room, "Doctor Mold, the two sick patients you have in Ward Thirteen have the same symptoms as mustard gas."

"Hey, that's it! Mustard Gas!"

"Doctor, what is mustard gas?"

"Oh, it's an oily liquid that was used to poison soldiers in World War I. It caused intense irritation of the mucous membranes and blistered the skin."

"Oh, but Doc, the weed killer I used on my yard was not oily at all!"

Another man walked into the room: "Yeah, Doctor, that's right. That weed killer isn't mustard gas. I just came from the science lab and they say it's not."

"For a minute there, I thought we were getting somewhere, but now I'm not so sure."

Mistress Mary's Mortal Magic Mischief

The next day, Doctor Mold and two scientists went to Melvin Mundy's house. They were wearing gas masks and air-tight protective suits. They began to pull on the milkweeds.

"Hey Doc, look, these weeds don't have milk in them."

"Yes, no sticky latex in the stems."

"But they do have an oily juice in them," noticed Melvin.

"Come on we've found the secret. Back to the lab, gentleman."

Back at the science laboratory, the scientists confirmed that the liquid in the plant stems was indeed mustard gas. They could now give an antidote to Mrs. Mundy and she would be fine. This is what the doctor had to say to sum up the story: "Someone created a substance that when sprayed on milkweed would change the milky latex to poisonous mustard gas."

THE END

I wonder who made that weed killer? Maybe the little old potion maker, Mistress Mary!"

So be careful whom you buy things from, it might be that Mistress Mary is up to no good. He he!

4. MONSTER MUSHROOMS

That last story reminded me about the time Mistress Mary made a strange potion she put in a city's water supply. It was in the summer and everyone was watering their gardens and their green lawns. Anyway, the potion made little mushroom plants grow six to ten feet tall! If any mushroom got wet, well, it would become a nice giant seat to sit on!

All over town, people were calling each other saying they had giant mushrooms in their yard. Can you imagine?

In one neighborhood, a baby was caught on top of a mushroom and the fire department was called in to help. They had to use a tall ladder to get the baby off the mushroom!

In another neighborhood, a house on posts was torn apart because mushrooms grew up under the house. Boy, that town was a mess! People spent weeks trying to saw up, chop up, and uproot these mushroom monstrosities. I bet Mistress Mary laughed the whole time! Ha ha, he he!

THE END

5. MAN-EATING MILLIPEDES

The "Man-eating Millipedes" is another story about one of Mary's magic potions. But this potion did not make the little worm-like millipedes grow to giant monsters. And it didn't make them have more legs than they already had. Instead, it made the millipedes have a very big appetite for human flesh. Yes, that's right, the millipedes would get on a human being and eat him in less than five minutes! These little insects terrified the community of Muskrat Maine until the citizens found out that only a few were actually man-eaters. The killers could be recognized by mysterious red spots on their backs. Eventually, the dangerous ones were killed off and the town was peaceful, quiet, and safe again. Mistress Mary had come real close to hurting herself because she had to stick the little millipedes in the back with a syringe (a sharp needle) and she almost stuck her own finger. I can't imagine what might have happened if she had gotten the potion in her own body! But she didn't, and she is still making new magic concoctions.

Read on...

6. MAD DOG MALARIA

Have you ever heard of a mad dog having rabies? Well, have you ever heard of a mad dog that had Malaria and carried it like a mosquito?

You haven't! Well then, I'll tell you now:

Mistress Mary put a spell on a mad dog that changed his rabies to Malaria. You can imagine what happened then. Yeah, the dog grew wings and began to fly around and pester people! But, he, thankfully, no longer barked!

You probably have noticed that the stories have been getting shorter. The main reason is because I am running out of room in this book. And the stories have gotten way too short so I'm now going to just write the titles...

A FEW TITLES

So have fun; you can make up your own stories with these titles.

7. MIDNIGHT'S MESSY MUD: Exactly at midnight, all mud changes to quicksand and people in rain-soaked muddy areas disappear during the night! So never go out after Mid-

night if it has rained recently!

8. MAD MINUTE MAID: A story about a new magic drink, not frozen orange juice or lemonade, but a tasty potion made by the mysterious Mistress Mary that takes only a minute to put a strange spell on you. What spell?

9. MURPHY'S MUSCULAR MUMPS: The ugly mumps get out of control and turn kids into big pimply faces. Oh no!

10. **And then there are these titles:**
(Write a story using one of these.)

The Mammoth Menacing Manikins
Moldy Meatballs and Mushy Melons
The Mysterious Mailbox Magpie
The Menacing Mummy Mutants
The Morbid Monkey Maze
The Mystical Magic Mirror
The Merry Motionless Man
The Miserable Melting Mix
March Marionette Madness
The Mean Monster Mantis
Midnight Mission to Mars
Marigolds In May
Mumbojumbo
Mum's Tums

Look, the titles have even gotten shorter!

So ends this book which couldn't have been written without MISTRESS MARY'S MORTAL MAGIC MISCHIEF.

Now that you have read this book, you can give it to another kid to read or tell them what kind of mischief Mistress Mary is up to, and be sure to tell him to watch out for milkweed and giant mushrooms.

—This last story was written by Donald Kirk in July of 1964 when he was 16 years old.

Hope you enjoyed the stories.
—Don Kirk